Christine Coleman, a University of Auckland graduate, practiced optometry in both Australia and New Zealand. Her other accomplishments include being a violinist with the New Zealand National Youth Orchestra, a singer with the Hamilton Operatic Society, an actress with the Mairangi Players, as well as a creditable pianist and bagpiper. Christine is a prolific short-story writer and lives in Auckland with her husband, Brian.

To my husband, Brian.

Christine Coleman

CONSPIRACY OF THE UNDEAD

A novel of intrigue, suspense, horror
and an ancient pagan folk dance

AUSTIN MACAULEY PUBLISHERS™

LONDON * CAMBRIDGE * NEW YORK * SHARJAH

Ordering Information
Quantity sales: Special discounts are available on quantity purchases by corporations, associations, and others. For details, contact the publisher at the address below.

Publisher's Cataloging-in-Publication data
Coleman, Christine
Conspiracy of the Undead

ISBN 9798889102434 (Paperback)
ISBN 9798889102441 (ePub e-book)

Library of Congress Control Number: 2023918111

www.austinmacauley.com/us

First Published 2024
Austin Macauley Publishers LLC
40 Wall Street, 33rd Floor, Suite 3302
New York, NY 10005
USA

mail-usa@austinmacauley.com
+1 (646) 5125767

Acknowledgment

Pat Coleman
Brian Bahlmann
Lloyd Bahlmann
Lel Crosthwaite-Scott
Brian Whitecliffe-Davies.

1

As far as pagan rituals go, there is nothing quite like the ancient annual rite of the Abbotts Bromley Horn Dance to stir the blood. Pagans young and old from far and wide congregate among curious non-pagans to immerse themselves in the Celtic heritage of 'The Horned One', Cernunnos, the god of fertility, life, animals, and the underworld.

One year from today, the Monday after the first Sunday of 4 September 1999 was to be no exception because a follower of the great Horned One would fall at the hands of one belonging to an even more powerful ancient cult. It had been pre-ordained that on this day, blood would be spilled upon the grounds of the village of Abbots Bromley. There would be a battle of sorts, but who was to be the survivor?

In the meantime, on the outskirts of the village, a young part-time art student by the name of Neville Yelavich was himself becoming a study in concentration. He was a slightly built twenty-five-year-old with rather too closely set eyes and a little goatee beard who liked nothing better than a challenge in life. He was preparing a sketch but despite his own self-protestations, was becoming more and more attracted to the new young model at his evening class. Her name was Caroline Mallory, a young teenage ingenue who was posing nude for pocket money. She was eighteen, in the full flush of youth and beautifully made up. Her long flaxen hair hung audaciously over one pristine alabaster shoulder and licking her lips, she fluttered her eyelashes alluringly in his direction.

He in turn, took a deep breath, gauged his angles and proportions with his B12 pencil held aloft, and began sketching with erratic concentration. How could this young fledgling with her snub nose and slightly crooked front teeth be making such an impression on him like this? She had a certain charm, a certain 'je ne sais quoi', which had the effect of drawing him to her in quite a literal sense. That naive shadow of a smile dancing over that studied pout flirted dangerously with his manhood. His sophistication and worldliness on the other hand were having a similar effect upon her.

He was a picture of self-control, never flinching in his dogged concentration while she herself struggled to contain her breathlessness, aware that if she moved a single muscle, she could end up quite contorted on canvas like some nu-vogue Picasso. The other half dozen students seemed unaware of the muted drama being played out under their eyes, or else were very cleverly concealing their intrigue…purely for the sake of upholding some kind of decorum in this stage-managed scene of course. After all, this young model was stark naked. Imagine if the spell of concentration were broken…. The young artist with the trademark goatee beard could throw down his pencil, thrust his easel aside, rip off all his clothes and rush recklessly into the arms of the naked model who would envelop him willingly to her heaving breast. Young love, or rather young lust, would have found its way.

Only a week of this study in sexual tension endured before Neville plucked up enough courage to introduce himself to Caroline to ask her out for coffee after class. Of this, they partook at the Elephant Café just ten minutes' walk away from the local high school where the art class was held. Caroline always remembered the place because of its excessively dingy interior and the pall of cigarette smoke that pervaded the place. It was definitely a place for artists to hang out. There were all sorts of pictures and other pertinent paraphernalia around the walls that looked like originals from the time of Clive of India when India was one of the colonies. There were paintings of elephants and suchlike everywhere. There was even a taxidermized elephant's foot hanging from the central ceiling like some huge prize lucky charm made into a tiffany lamp with a light bulb half inside it and long gold tassels hanging from its toenails. All the smoke seemed to accumulate there under the center light like a mist hanging over an Indian swamp.

Neville and Caroline soon became an item and hung out everywhere together. They were like a young Darby and Joan. Within two months, they were engaged. They even took a week's holiday to Ireland together. Then, just as suddenly as the relationship started, it was over. It was as if it were fate. Caroline had met someone else. Neville couldn't figure it out. Here he was, a reasonably handsome amateur artist, tennis player and Morris dancer with a good job at the hospital in Derby, ousted by some down and out unemployed Irish roustabout. It just didn't make sense.

To compensate for his loss, Neville buried himself in his art and turned out some quite creative avant-garde-looking works of nude women in various poses, but his favorite ones, of course, were of Caroline. His sketches of her remained immortalized on canvas in bright gouache and thick oil paint, the ripeness of her youth being preserved forever. Often, he would stand in front of his last painting of her and brood incessantly. He would become almost mesmerized by the startling colors of his own creation as if in some kind of trance. It was as if she still held some kind of spell over him.

*

A year passed by and the auspicious day arrived. Down through a low stone-walled lane leading into the main street of the quaint black and white half-timbered village of Abbots Bromley, a neo-Gothic seraphic-looking blonde creature clad in a diaphanous floral skirt and leather jacket sidled up to her even more incongruous looking boyfriend dressed in heavy metal duds and studs and turned up their ghetto blaster. The old song, 'Only Women Bleed' blurted out its whining symphony for all and sundry to hear. Outside this little microcosm, a carnival atmosphere pervaded the air. There were various craft stalls and organizations displaying their wares on the village green and underneath the Buttercross. The five village pubs had had a very busy night as expected during the night before.

People of all shapes and sizes, colors and creeds, blithely followed the leather-clad young couple to a vantage point across the moat from Blithfield Hall. The horn dancers had been invited to dance there for Lady Bagot and her guests before lunch on the front lawn. Louise Mallory, a neophyte grandmother with an interest in dance (as an ex-ballet dancer) was among the spectators overlooking the moat. She was a petite forty-year-old happily married lady with beautiful skin, who looked far too young to be a grandmother and who had a new lease on life now that she had retired from ballet. Ballet had always been the be-all and end-all for her, but now the boot was on the other foot.

She had come along today to cheer on her husband, Victor, the lead deerman, who held the heaviest of the horns. The horn dance was, of course, a specialized type of Morris dance using antlers mounted over the shoulders. (These particular antlers had been carbon dated at over nine hundred years old.) The horn dance was a dance traditionally only ever danced by men.

"Whoever heard of a female Morris dancer?" Louise overhead a male voice in the crowd ask pointedly.

"That's almost as bad as being a male nun!" another smart Alec male voice quipped.

A group guffaw ricocheted around the surrounding crowd and then there was an immediate hush. The dance troupe has just jumped out of their van and crossed the moat into the Hall grounds. The dancers had been spared some of the twenty-mile hike today by a sympathetic admirer driving past in his four-wheel drive Land Rover.

There was a short confabulation among the dancers and then the accordion and triangle players started up the well-known 'Robinson Tune', signaling the commencement of the dance. It was a sprightly tune reminiscent of horses clip-clopping their way along cobbled curb stones. The dancers lined up and began circling and chaining in their quasi-medieval costumes, antlers held aloft upon the shoulders of the six deermen. There was a sharp shout and they formed into a set of five a side. This included a young Robin Hood as the bowman, a Maid Marion (a man dressed up as a woman), a jester and a hobbyhorse. Each time the bowman came face to face with the hobbyhorse, his arrow was scraped across his bow with a menacing twang so that the hobbyhorse reacted with a clacking of its articulated jaw. When the intonation of the music changed, the three pairs of deermen challenged each other by lightly clashing antlers, while the other two pairs of characters thrust their hands forward and up at each other. Another shout signaled a crossing over between the two lines. This sequence was repeated several times to the music and then the lead deerman would lead off to begin the dance again.

Louise Mallory had brought a young friend with her today. She was a young lady by the name of Elspeth Glossop from the Sadlers Wells Ballet company. She was a strawberry blonde woman with extremely full jowls, unusual to see in one so young and especially in a ballet dancer. You could almost say that she had the face and neck of a swan, with such high cheekbones and elegant neck. But her figure was delectable, typical of that found in a ballerina, and she moved with a certain grace that could not be denied. It was her elegant bearing and no-nonsense manner that grabbed your attention upon first meeting. Both she and Louise had a keen interest in traditional and folk dance. Elspeth, for one, taught folk dancing privately to primary school children in her spare time.

"My gosh, Elspeth," said Louise, "I do hope my Victor's going to last the distance today. He's been feeling a bit under the weather for the past month. Very tired, you know. But then he is getting on a bit. We both are. We're grandparents now, you know. We can't keep up with you young ones like we used to."

"Yes, I suppose it catches up with us all eventually," said Elspeth. "But he certainly looks the part in that headgear. He's such a big strapping man. Makes him look like he's the real leader of the pack, or should I say, herd?"

"Yes, I think he makes a far better deerman than he would a Maid Marion, doesn't he? So tall and rugged and masculine!"

As soon as she uttered those words, Louise had immediate misgivings. She and Victor had a little secret. Victor was a closet cross-dresser. In fact, she knew that Victor would have made a perfect Maid Marion. Certainly, better than the one they had. If Victor had had the part, he would have ended up looking more like a woman dressed as a woman…only an extremely tall and well-built woman. He was so particular when he came out 'en femme'. But of course, that was only at night and only once a month, not just once a year on the Monday after the first Sunday after September 4th.

So, Victor, when he put his mind to it, was really more like a beautiful nocturnal moth compared to this diurnal Maid Marion's poor attempt at a butterfly. Mind you, the quasi-medieval costuming did nothing for any of the dancers really. All the trousers had forty-inch waists with drawstring waistbands so their figures could not be sartorially enhanced with a particularly tailored look.

To her relief, Elspeth seemed not to dwell on Louise's comment. To Elspeth, Victor seemed more like a Viking, as he was hugely tall with sandy hair and a big gruff voice. She could even imagine him wearing a horned helmet as a Valkyrie in a Wagnerian opera if she thought about it, but then again, she thought he probably looked less formidable as a deerman in quasi-medieval dress. Then changing the subject, she said, "That jester is really dainty on his feet, isn't he? So agile. Born to the part."

"Yes, that's Neville Yelavich," replied Louise. "He used to be engaged to our daughter, Caroline. For some strange reason, the wedding was canceled two weeks before it was due to go ahead. I'll never understand why Caroline ran off with Albert Pengally to Ireland."

"Really?"

"Yes, Neville's such a clever lad. Albert tends to come across as the exact opposite, even though he's four years older than Neville."

"How strange."

"Yes…these things happen," she sighed. "Anyway, Elspeth, I'm glad you came over to spot the local talent. You never know when the next Nureyev is going to show up do you?"

Elspeth smiled. As a relative newcomer to the Sadlers Wells Ballet, she was eager to explore all avenues of dance, even the avant-garde type and especially traditional and folk. So, she had been especially pleased when her ballet mistress had put her in touch with Louise, as Louise actually had one of her very own family members involved in this ancient horn dance today.

Elspeth had arrived from London the previous evening and the Mallorys had taken her out to a Sunday pub meal to get her fully-versed in the background and history of the dance.

"Now then, young Elspeth," Victor had said in his gruff voice. "We he-men don't do pirouettes and that type of stuff like you do. You will see tomorrow that we do a lot of walking and a few semi-high kicks."

Louise interrupted. "Oh, he means 'hops', Elspeth. I don't think any of them would be capable of 'high kicks'."

Victor opened his mouth at Louise and then carried on.

"Yes, well, those bloody antlers weigh a bloody ton. My ones weigh twenty-five pounds!"

"Yes love. I'll let you off the high kicks then."

"I should think so. None of us blokes are ballet dancers…or even body builders, come to think of it. I bet she didn't tell you that, did she, Elspeth? Louise is far too modest. But she's taken up body building since she gave up ballet and she's even won a few cups, haven't you dear? Show Elspeth some of your muscles, pet."

Louise lowered her eyes coyly and said, "I'm sure Elspeth isn't interested in my pectorals."

"Oh yes, Louise. Do show me," Elspeth piped up excitedly.

With that, Louise unbuttoned her jacket, rolled up one sleeve and posed with one arm bent, 'strong-man' fashion and with a pneumatic roll of the tongue went, "Grrrr!"

Elspeth was impressed. "You do that so well!" she said.

"Well now that I'm no longer dancing, I need something to keep me occupied and ship-shape, and body building is it."

"What a great idea."

"Yes, something for every ballet dancer to contemplate when they retire. Put it in your diary for later on," she said airily.

Elspeth grinned.

Victor took a deep breath. "Anyway, as I was saying Elspeth…now, where was I? Oh yes, the history of the horn dance. That's what you're interested in isn't it, you yourself being originally from Perthshire I hear, where they don't do this type of thing?"

Elspeth nodded expectantly and then shook her head.

"Well, many years ago, before you or I or Louise were born…in fact, thousands of years ago back in the Stone Age, men with bows and arrows used to stalk other men wearing animal skins and head-dresses. They used to mime a successful hunt as a symbolic empowerment over an actual quarry. There are cave paintings in France and Derbyshire showing this. In France, they date back to 20,000 B.C. and in Derbyshire to 12,000 B.C. Then in Yorkshire, they found antler frontlets dated to around 7,600 B.C. They reckon the horn dance originated with the extinction of reindeer in Britain and the ritual dance of the deermen was to incite an increase in the herds to ensure survival of the tribes."

Louise butted in. "Victor has a real head for figures. Typical accountant."

Elspeth grinned and Victor carried on, ignoring the innuendo of Louise's offhand remark. He had already mentally assessed Elspeth's assets, figuratively speaking, thank you very much.

"The dance was first performed in Staffordshire around 1,125 A.D, when the foresters bought the hunting rights in Needwood Forest from the Abbot of Bromley so as to restore their Saxon privileges. And it always used to be performed in August around the winter solstice, but nowadays it's always performed on Wakes Monday in September."

"Interesting," said Elspeth.

"You'll notice in the dance," Victor went on, "that Robin Hood, the bowman, pretends to shoot the hobbyhorse. That's sort of symbolic of Celtic-Saxon horse worship. And at the end of the dance, the bowman symbolically stakes the six deermen with his arrows and they all lie down and 'die', symbolic of a successful hunt. The combat between the three black and three white horned deermen symbolizes death and rebirth, just as the natural annual shedding of a male deer's antlers represents a seasonal dying and re-growth. Maid Marion represents fertility and the jester represents adversity or, I suppose, you'd call it the luck of the hunt."

"How fascinating," said Elspeth.

"Yes, nowadays," Louise added, "Maid Marion collects alms for St Nicholas's Church in the ladle that she carries. Interestingly enough, the emblem of St Nicholas's Church is the stag."

"That's right," said Victor. "And the dancers bring good luck and fertility to all within the twenty-mile circuit that we cover."

"Oh, that's nice," said Elspeth. "I could do with some of that. Good luck, that is. So basically, the horn dance represents the survival of a Stone Age pagan ritual combined with elements of forest law and Morris dancing."

"In a nutshell, yes, I suppose you could say that," said Victor. "A deer running ceremony of sorts. We start at eight o'clock tomorrow morning. We have to collect the horns from the church, get changed and attend a quick service first."

"Now that you mention it," said Elspeth, "it does seem rather strange that the remnants of a pagan festival are kept within the hallowed walls of a Christian church."

"Yes, I suppose it does. All I can tell you is that there was an annual fair, Barthelmy Fair, held in the town since being granted that right by Henry III in 1226. The Wakes Festival is a direct descendant of this fair. Then, in the 1300s, the church was dedicated to St Nicholas, whose symbol is the reindeer. The antlers, at that time being two-hundred-year-old curiosities, were probably used to collect funds for the upkeep of the church to provide for the poor during the Wakes Festival. The antlers probably became such a successful money-making device that the head masks were added to improve them a little. So, there you are…money talks!"

"Fancy that! Even back in those days," said Elspeth. She pondered the matter a little and then asked, "So where are you off to after you've picked up the horns tomorrow morning?"

"After that, we're off to the village green, Gooselane, Yeatsall Farm…dancing in driveways along the way. We get lunch at Blithfield Hall, courtesy of Lady Bagot (she always feeds us well), and then we're off to Little Dunstall Farm, Rugeley Turn, the Bagot Arms…everywhere…and back to the village green again by eight o'clock at night. And, of course, we have a few pub stops along the way."

"Not forgetting that…" said Louise with much alacrity.

"Sounds great!" said Elspeth.

"A bit exhausting, but it's all good fun," said Victor.

"Yes, well just mind you have a good breakfast, dear," said Louise. "I don't want you exhausting yourself like you have been during the last few practice nights."

"I'll be okay."

"I hope so. You came back looking as white as a sheet after your last practice."

"Don't worry love. I wouldn't do it if I didn't enjoy it."

"I know."

Louise looked helplessly at Elspeth as if to say, "What else can I do?"

Changing the subject, Victor suddenly sat up straight and waved across the room to a fellow Morris dancer. It was the hobby horseman, alias the handsome young Larry Johnson. Larry was a boyish-faced young man in his thirties going prematurely gray at the temples which strangely seemed to add to his allure as far as the opposite sex was concerned. He had the most devastatingly long eyelashes, which framed the most devilishly handsome brown eyes you could ever imagine. It was a wonder he hadn't been snaffled by some inveigling woman's charms already, but then again perhaps he was enjoying playing the field too much.

"Hello there, Ol' Dobbin! Come on over!"

Victor waved Larry across to the table. In an aside to Elspeth, he said, "Someone you might like to meet, Elspeth. You're not spoken for, are you?"

Elspeth shook her head from side to side, her strawberry blonde hair flirting outrageously with her high cheekbones.

*

The next morning was fine and crisp. They could not have asked for a better day. Elspeth had her camera with her and arrived on the Mallorys' front doorstep just after 8am. Victor had already left after having eaten a substantial breakfast of bacon and eggs, toast and marmalade, and a hot buttered savory muffin, followed by strong coffee. Louise had made sure of that.

"Come in, Elspeth. Would you like a coffee before we go?"

"No thanks, Louise. I'm full to the brim with coffee. Larry plied me with umpteen coffees after you and Victor left last night."

"Oh, so there's something going on now, is there?"

"No, not really. We were just being sociable."

"That's what they all say." She smiled knowingly. "I see you've got your camera with you. Great. It's a perfect day out there. You should get some good shots. I'm bringing my camera, too."

The two women drove off in Elspeth's old Buick to the village green and arrived there by 8.30 am. A small crowd was beginning to gather on the village green and the two pubs which overlooked it had already opened their doors. Elspeth and Louise put their shoulder bags down behind where a family group was standing nearby when they were startled by a sudden roar from overhead. It was a quintet of RAF Tornadoes bearing down on them on what they assumed was a practice run. Or was it a celebratory stunt to start the day off with a hiss and a roar? They weren't too sure. However, a little disconcerted, they were soon craning their necks to watch the horn dancers who had by now arrived.

The music started up and the two women at once began tapping their feet. Not quite ballet music, but it was definitely music that made you feel like dancing. Elspeth immediately noticed 'Ol' Dobbin' there, dressed in his finery and making a spectacle of himself. He looked none the worse for wear after all that coffee the night before. Probably made him even more sprightly. She raised her camera above the heads of the crowd in front and aimed hopefully in Dobbin's direction. Just as she clicked the shutter, the man in front hoisted his young son onto his shoulders, ruining her shot. "Damn!" she said softly, realizing they would have to find a better viewing spot. She nudged Louise and they moved a little further to the left, where there was a slight gap in the crowd. Through the gap, Elspeth caught sight of Robin Hood and was amazed to see that he was a mere youth of about fourteen or fifteen. He was tall and lanky, but well-coordinated and had a bad case of acne on his face. "Oh, that's traditional," said Louise. "Robin Hood is always a young person. Don't ask me why. I think it's something to do with youth outlasting old age. Victor would know."

"Well, he's very good. He seems to be giving Larry a hard time as the hobby horse."

"Yes, he seems to be enjoying it, doesn't he? Wait till he gets to kill all the old stags. One of the deermen is his dad, Trevor. That's him…the short guy with the bushy sideburns. He really likes sticking his arrow into him! A bit of the old tit for tat, I suppose. You know, the old father/son thing. Gabriel likes to get his own back!"

"Oh."

There was a slight pause and an embarrassed giggle. Then Elspeth remarked, "Look at that jester fellow with the coxcomb! He's so quick! He reminds me of Sir Robert Helpman playing Fagin in *Oliver Twist*. He really plays up to the crowd too, doesn't he? And he seems to be getting under Victor's feet a lot too, I notice."

"Yes, that's Neville again," said Louise. "That's his job. He's supposed to clown around and be a little bit of a trouble-maker. He's good at it isn't he? But the rest of the dancers are supposed not to notice."

"Yes, Victor's being very stoical about it isn't he?" said Elspeth.

"Yes, sometimes I think Victor would just like to stop and yell at him, 'You bloody fool! Why don't you mind where you're going?' But I don't think it would do him any good!" Louise laughed.

The dancers kept doggedly on with their circling and snaking up the green until the music stopped. The crowd immediately clapped and cheered in appreciation. Then, because they couldn't let the opportunity go by of two open pubs on a hot day, the dancers gently planted their horns upon the ground and went inside to quench their thirst, Gabriel tagging along behind his dad. The crowd kept a respectful distance from the black and white tipped antlers, which had now taken on the appearance of a tableau of oddly pruned rose bushes, their branches every which way in supplication to the sky.

Once fortified with a little sustenance, the dancers were on their way again, this time to Goose Lane. They led off in single file, antlers aloft, with Victor in front like the Pied Piper of Hamlin, while the crowd fell in behind them, following like a host of rats hypnotized by the music of his magic pipes. They paraded like this through the streets of Abbots Bromley until they reached Goose Lane just after nine o'clock. Here, there were even more spectators gathered around waiting for them, eager to witness this maybe once-in-a-lifetime event for some. The atmosphere was charged with expectancy and goodwill as the dancers approached. The familiar 'clip-clopping' music struck up and Victor and his Morris dancing squad were immediately in their element.

They recommenced the centuries-old dance routine with renewed vim and vigor. They had it off pat to such a degree that it was almost as if they themselves had been practicing for centuries. The crowd was impressed and rallied their support.

The performances were repeated throughout the day, the ecstatic crowds following behind getting bigger and bigger. Sometimes the dancers hoodwinked their admirers by hitch-hiking a ride down a side street with some sympathetic motorist, so shaking some of them off. But their admirers always caught up with them in the end, if a little puffed. When they came to young Gabriel Taylor's front driveway, the young Robin Hood gallantly let his mother have a turn with his bow and arrow. This she gleefully did, cavorting with his feathered hat perched on her head and aiming at imaginary birds in the trees in front of all the spectators. She was a real sport.

By the time they got to Blithfield Hall, the dancers had all worked up quite an appetite. However, instead of singing for their supper, they had to dance. They arrived just on twelve o'clock to the cheering of even more spectators and jumped out of the four-wheel-drive whose driver had taken pity on them having to walk all the way. Each dancer made the acquaintance of Lady Bagot, a most gracious elderly lady and then once the introductions were over, they began their dance.

There was much cheering and clapping afterward from the crowds watching from across the moat, and also from Lady Bagot and her guests on the lawn. One of her guests, an elderly gentleman from Yorkshire with a distinguished-looking handlebar mustache, was overheard saying to his wife, who was an equally distinguished-looking lady, "We should get them to come up and perform this in Yorkshire each time before a fox hunt. Might make some sort of difference…you never know…"

His wife glared at him patently unamused. Obviously, an animal lover at loggerheads with her spouse.

It was now time for the dancers to lay down their horns and partake of a little lunch. Lunch at Lady Bagot's was always spectacular. Cucumber sandwiches laid out on little paper doilies on long white trestle tables, together with savory muffins, asparagus rolls, little pigs-in-blankets, devils on horseback, cheese and bacon hors d'oeuvres, strawberry cream butterfly cakes, chocolate eclairs and pavlova. Then there was tea or coffee if you preferred.

Needless to say, the dancers called for no encouragement to get stuck into this mouth-watering spread. They each loaded their plates and then sat down appreciatively on the specially provided colored deck chairs set out under the green and white striped sun umbrellas pegged out on the lawn. Victor loaded up his plate with goodies, collected a cup of tea and parked himself in a deck chair next to Trevor Taylor.

"By golly," said Victor, looking slightly harassed. "I need this grub."

He bit hungrily into his savory muffin and chewed thoughtfully. After a few swallows, he started to feel more at ease. Then he said to Trevor musingly, "Is it just me, or do you too find that when Neville's around playing the fool under your feet that you get very tired?"

"Can't say I've noticed it mate. Neville's always getting in the way. He'd get on anyone's nerves."

"It's just that at practice lately, whenever Neville gets under my feet, I've got home extremely tired. It's really weird."

"That does sound weird."

"I try not to notice him, but it doesn't seem to help. He's always around somewhere."

"Oh mate, you've got to be imagining it. You've probably just got low blood sugar or something…especially if you're feeling better now that you've had something to eat. You look all right to me at the moment."

"Yes, but have you noticed? Neville's way down the opposite end of the garden there."

"Nah, I'd say it's your blood sugar. Try a piece of that pavlova. It looks delicious. It's my boy Gabriel who gets on my nerves…especially when he's firing that bloody bow and arrow at me…but I cope. There's nothing a little pavlova won't fix," he said as he lifted a huge spoonful of the fluffy stuff into his mouth, his eyes closing in ecstasy as he slowly devoured it.

Victor watched, almost embarrassed by his friend's enjoyment and then, somewhat encouraged, did likewise, glancing nervously in Neville's direction as he did so. He hoped Trevor was right. Perhaps it was just his blood sugar…

His attention was diverted just then as several of the spectators crossed over the moat holding special passes. Among them was a lady from BBC Radio 4 and a small camera crew who were making a TV pilot film on ancient rituals.

"Uh-oh!" he said. "It looks like we're in for a couple of interviews."

He hurriedly swallowed his last mouthful and slapped any crumbs off his hands. He needn't have been quite so hasty however, as both interviewers were making their way toward Lady Bagot.

The Bagots of course had been living on the old Blithfield estate since the fourteenth century. Within the landscaped gardens were a church, a museum, an eighteenth-century orangery and the descendants of a herd of black bearded white goats given to Sir John Bagot by King Richard II. (The ancestors of these goats were said to have been taken from the Rhine Valley to Palestine on one of the Crusades and were brought back to England as traveling food.)

Blithfield Hall itself was an ancient ivy-clad mansion with embattled towers and walls, giving it the appearance of a huge fortress. One of the old oak trees on the estate was said to be seventy feet tall and stood as straight as a die, hence its name; 'Bagot's Walking Stick'.

Victor watched with some interest as the camera crew ran a few films through of Lady Bagot being interviewed over lunch. The lady from BBC Radio 4 was interviewing some of the guests. She was an extremely attractive blonde dressed in a beautifully-fitting crimson suit, with a short skirt exhibiting a pair of very shapely legs. The only flaw to her good looks was a slightly receding forehead which, when viewed in profile along with her cosmetically augmented lips, gave her a strangely fishlike appearance. Vaguely, Victor wondered if she might be related to a family by the name of Fishlock that he once knew when suddenly the lady in question headed his way.

"Hello. My name's Mellissa Wright from BBC Radio 4. You're the head deerman, I believe?"

"Yes, that's right," said Victor, somewhat deferentially. "Take a seat," he said, indicating the empty deck chair on his right.

"Thank you. Now, we are doing a program on 'Open Country' and would love to hear it not from the horse's mouth, but from the mouth of the leading stag. Would you like to enlighten us?"

"Well, thank you. I am honored, I must say. Obviously today is a lot of fun for everyone involved, especially the participants…that's us, the horn dancers. We practice once a week throughout the year and the culmination of all this work—and play—is what you see today. We hugely enjoy it; the pageantry, the history, the appreciation of the crowds and all the refreshments on hand…and the extra hours that the pubs stay open!"

"Of course. I'm sure they appreciate all the extra custom as well."

She re-crossed her elegant legs and tossed her hair.

"Now, Mr. Mallory," she began. "I wonder if you would mind telling me the significance of the black and white tipped antlers and deer masks. Is there a reason for the two different colors?"

"Yes, well the ritual combat between the two teams of black and white represents the conflict between light and darkness, spring and winter, and death and rebirth—just like how a deer's antlers are annually shed and regrown, I suppose. The three white horns always lead off when we're in single file."

"I see. Isn't it amazing to think that those antlers are almost one thousand years old? And they're kept in St Nicholas's Church, aren't they? A most incongruous place for keeping pagan relics, I must say. But I understand that with St Nicholas's emblem being a stag, the horn dance was used as a way of collecting alms for the church and raising money for the poor."

"That's right."

Miss Wright tossed her hair again and carried on.

"So, you have belonged to the Abbots Bromley Morris Dancing Club for how long, Mr. Mallory?"

"Er, about ten years."

"And your day job?"

"I'm an accountant, but I'm not one of the old schools. I do use a computer."

"Well, that's an interesting combination. A gentleman here," she said to her audience over the microphone, "who has a distinct merger of both ancient and modern interests."

She glanced toward Trevor on Victor's right and asked, "And this gentleman here sitting next to you?"

"Oh, this is Trevor Taylor. He's the second deerman. He carries white tipped horns as well."

"Oh, lovely!"

She leaned toward Trevor in her low-cut jacket and said, "Now tell me, Mr. Taylor, about those costumes you're wearing."

Trevor fingered the top button of his jerkin and stammered, "Oh, these were supplied by Lord and Lady Bagot. They're based on the Berkley costume of the early 1900s—breeches, stockings, sleeveless jerkins as you can see, and a cap."

"Mmm. Very dapper."

Mellissa Wright moved down the line of deckchairs, guilelessly displaying her womanly wares as she went. It was her flashy pair of legs that seemed to get the most attention. She gave short interviews to each of the dancers in turn, including young Maid Marion, a swarthy, curly-haired young man, to whom she said, "Maid Marion, I presume? Who put you in that dreadful dress? You look all kind of saggy-baggy. I wish I had a few spare safety pins on me! I could work wonders for you—honest!"

"Oh no," he stammered. "Don't touch me, I'm okay."

He sank back into the depths of his deck chair, somewhat in awe of this extremely attractive woman, especially as his girlfriend was no doubt watching his every move from over the moat.

"Oh, I suppose you're comfortable in that outfit. That's what counts I suppose, when you've got all that walking to do from place to place."

Maid Marion blushed because so far, they had had three lifts along the way.

"Well, let me know any time if you ever need a little hitching up," Miss Wright went on.

Self-consciously, Maid Marion looked down at his costume and adjusted his waistband.

Upon reaching Neville at the far end of the row of deck chairs, Mellissa Wright took a step back, obviously impressed with his costume.

"And here we have the jester!"

Neville sat up as straight as he could in his deck chair and looked alert. He was bright-eyed, slightly-built, ambidextrous and double-jointed. One corner of his multifaceted jester's cap hung slightly over one eye, jingling as he spoke.

"Pleased to meet you, Miss."

"And you, Sir. I say, do you enjoy playing the fool?"

"Of course. I love it," said Neville, waving his coxcomb with aplomb.

"I've been watching you during the dance. You're very fleet of foot."

"I was born to it. It's because I'm so clever you see."

"You're certainly very agile. You're kind of everywhere at once."

"Thank you."

"So, what do you do when you're not playing the fool?"

"Oh, I'm a lab technician at the blood bank in Derby."

"And what blood group are you?"

"Blue."

"But of course, you are. How stupid of me!"

She smiled and turned away for a moment to speak to her audience on air through her microphone. The sun cast golden glints in her blonde hair as she spoke of the grandeur of Blithfield Hall, the surroundings and what the crowds were up to over the moat. Her obvious good looks, perfect grooming and magnetic personality held the crowd's interest over the moat so that, once she had finished speaking to her studio audience, to her surprise, she was given a short clap. Accordingly, she took a bow before re-conferring with her two recording assistants who were hovering close by.

Once that little item was over, the dancers helped themselves to seconds from the long trestle tables before preparing to leave for the next venue. The film crew still seemed to be concentrating on Lady Bagot and the magnificent architecture of the hall, so there was little likelihood of the dancers being troubled by further interviews for the moment.

*

Little Dunstall Farm was next on the agenda, followed by Rugeley Turn, The Bagot Arms (time for a pint), the Royal Oak, The Goat's Head, The Crown Inn (and time for another pint). It was when Victor was ordering a quick pint at The Crown that Neville came up to him at the bar.

"How're you doing, Vic? Bearing up?"

"Yeah. Fine, mate. What're you having?"

"Bloody Mary, thanks, mate."

"Right you are. Coming up."

Neville was standing right next to Victor at the bar when suddenly Victor didn't feel so well. He grabbed a bar stool and sat down. Sweat started to form in tiny beads upon his forehead.

"You all right, mate?" asked Neville. "You look as white as a sheet. You're probably better off with a bit of grub inside you. How about one of those filled rolls over there?"

Victor nodded.

"I'll be back in a sec," said Neville and went to buy a roll.

As soon as he had gone, Victor started to feel a little better. What was it with Neville? It was as if his energy was being sapped in his presence. This was weird. When Neville returned with the roll, Victor naturally offered to pay for it.

"No, it's on me, mate. Every ex-prospective father-in-law deserves a free lunch now and then. Now get that down ya."

Neville patted his ex-prospective father-in-law on the shoulder and sat down to sip his Bloody Mary which had now arrived. Victor, who was still feeling slightly faint, managed to do justice to the filled roll well enough. He had always liked and admired Neville for his manners and intelligence and would have welcomed him with open arms as a son-in-law. He had a good steady job, was well-liked by his peers, played at the local tennis club, was a wee bit too arty for him he had to admit, but at least he Morris-danced and that was a big plus in Victor's eyes. Any male who appreciated history and tradition enough to practice it had to be a good bloke. What more could you ask for in a son-in-law? But it was not to be. His daughter, Caroline, had run away to Ireland and married someone else.

"Thanks for the filled roll, Neville."

"No worries, mate. Thanks for the drink."

*

Friendship restored once more, they were soon off to Schoolhouse Lane, Bagot's View, Radmore Lane, Lichfield Road, The Coach and Horses, and then High Street, the main street, before making it back to the village green in the early evening. Victor noticed that the film crew had kept up with them all the way and would very likely be filming again at their next stop in the village green if there was still enough light before they took the horns back to the church.

At High Street, Victor led the team off as usual in time to the music, but it was a little more cramped for space because of the crowds crammed in on both sides of the street. A larger crowd had gathered than expected and the local policemen and their reinforcements were struggling to maintain traffic control nearby. The light was fading and the sun was sinking low toward the horizon in the south-west. Several windows from nearby shop fronts were catching the light and dazzling some of the bystanders, disturbing their view. Not to mention the view of the dancers who had more than a few minor obstacles to contend with in such a cramped space.

The music started up and the dancers began. They began as they had always done, circling to the music, advancing and receding, clashing horns and crossing over. But just as Victor was about to lead off again, there was some interference from the audience. A small but well-built and obstreperous child in the front row with ice cream smeared all over his face was licking the last remnants from his cone in a rather provocative manner. He was standing with a restraining lead fastened around his chest and tied to the empty pushchair beside him. His parents, standing behind him, were engrossed in the dance. Neville, the jester, made a face at the child, as any good jester would. But taking this as a challenge, the naughty child girded his loins, lunged forward toward Neville and made a grab for his coxcomb with his pushchair trailing behind.

Taken by surprise, Neville was thrown off balance as he took evasive action and barged into Victor, hitting him unavoidably with his coxcomb. Neville, being so lightweight, was flung bodily away by Victor's turning horns and Victor's interrupted momentum caused him to twist off balance. As fate would have it, Victor came down hard upon a couple of cobblestones and careered into the pushchair—still attached to the runaway child—causing him to ricochet at an awkward angle back on top of Neville, supine on the ground. Neville took the full force of Victor and the antlers so that he effectively became skewered to the ground as if by a corkscrewing pitchfork.

The child immediately stood stock still. Blood spurted from Neville's stomach. It had all happened so fast.

There was a bellowing scream from Neville and a collective gasp from the crowd. Blood began to ooze from between the folds of Neville's costume where he had been gored. He lay wincing in pain on the ground like an insect stuck by a pin, only with one arm and both legs moving. Victor lay on top of him, antlers still in his grip, and breathing hotly upon Neville's neck. Victor was feeling very faint and couldn't move. He was a dead weight upon Neville's chest.

The music stopped.

"Quick! Get a doctor!" someone yelled.

A man rushed forward from the crowd. Neville was still writhing on the ground in pain which, unfortunately, corkscrewed the antler even further into his stomach.

"Get back! Get back! I'm a doctor," shouted the man, kneeling beside the stricken pair.

The crowd eased forward to take a closer look.

"I need three strong men!" the doctor yelled.

Three volunteers stepped forward.

"We've got to get this big guy off the little guy. But first, I'll loosen his grip on the antlers, okay?"

"Okay."

The three men gently eased Victor, who was now out cold, off Neville while the doctor supervised. Then the doctor tried to unscrew two antler tips from Neville's stomach while the three men held him down. Neville was just about frothing at the mouth.

The doctor paused.

"Okay, we need an ambulance and possibly a saw," he said.

2

The headlines in the local newspapers the next day went something like, 'NINE-HUNDRED-YEAR-OLD ANTLERS MUTILATED TO SAVE MORRIS DANCER'S LIFE'. All the locals were aghast and the national historians were horrified. A little piece of history had been made and it was the buzz of the town. The Abbots Bromley Horn Dance would never be the same again with one pair of severed horns. Even Superglue or some such thing might not be enough, as the horns had to be clashed together during the dance.

When Victor came to at the scene of the accident, he could faintly hear the sound of an ambulance siren receding into the distance. Then there was the unmistakable, higher-pitched crescendo of a second ambulance approaching. This one was for him. Two paramedics helped him aboard a stretcher and he was put inside the van.

"Just to be on the safe side, sir. We don't know if you just fainted, or if there is some underlying condition. Stay lying down now, there's a good chap."

Victor did as he was told and within a good twenty minutes they were at the hospital in Derby where coincidentally, Neville happened to work. Victor was put in a wheelchair and wheeled into an anteroom. Soon he was being examined by an intern in a white coat and being asked several searching questions such as when did he last eat, what medications was he on and had he ever felt faint before etc. Then he was immediately sent down to the lab for hematology tests and analysis before being kept in overnight for observation. Meanwhile, Neville was in intensive care being drip-fed after having had the antler tips sawn off and unscrewed from his stomach and been given an emergency blood transfusion. Luckily, they had all the information regarding his blood type (B for blue) at their fingertips as he was on their staff list at the hospital. He was in a very critical condition and needed around-the-clock surveillance. There was no point in taking any X-rays until his condition had stabilized however.

Victor slowly started to feel better and after a nice cup of tea and a biscuit from one of the nurses, his color gradually started to return.

"I don't suppose I could have another of those delicious peanut brownies, nurse?" he asked.

"Of course, Mr. Mallory. Have as many as you like. More tea?"

Victor nodded and tucked in.

"Oh, your wife and daughter have just arrived to see you Mr. Mallory."

"My daughter? My daughter's in Ireland."

Just then Louise and her friend Elspeth entered the room, both looking very concerned.

"How are you love?" Louise asked. "I've brought Elspeth along for moral support."

Elspeth smiled encouragingly.

"I'm fine," said Victor. "Feeling a lot better. It's these peanut brownies you see," he grinned.

"You still look a little pale love. They've run tests, have they?" asked Louise.

"Yes. Still waiting for the results."

"Have you heard how Neville is?" Elspeth asked.

"Not too good, apparently. I feel terrible about it. But I just couldn't let go of the horns!"

"Oh dear. Let's hope he picks up," said Louise. "Elspeth and I saw it all happen. It was just a freak accident, wasn't it, Elspeth? If that little kid had been kept under parental control, none of this would have happened. What is it with some parents today? They just don't seem to care, do they? That little brute should have been in his pushchair, tied in, preferably, and his parents should have been hanging firmly onto it. I was always very particular with Caroline when she was little and we were out in public. She was always under control."

"Yes love. You were a very good mother," Victor conceded.

Elspeth smiled and then said, "Did you know that the film crew caught all the action on film? Apparently, they've been running action replays of the exact sequence of events, according to the papers, to work out how it all happened. They're doing a slow-motion analysis."

"Well, I must say," said Louise, "it would be an absolutely unrepeatable event. It would need split second timing if they wanted to choreograph it for a new ballet."

Elspeth let out a guffaw.

"I doubt they'd get anyone stupid enough to audition!" she said.

"Unless they were paid the Earth," said Louise.

"Yes, there's that," Elspeth admitted ruefully.

"So, how's the little boy?" Victor asked.

"Oh, he's okay," said Louise, "but his parents are quite upset. According to one of the nurses out there, they're coming in later today to offer their condolences to both you and Neville. They'll be leaving all their children with a sitter, by the way, so that's good news for you. Apparently, they've got three; the four-year-old and twins of eighteen months. So just warning you, you'd better be on your best behavior."

"Of course. What do you take me for?"

Louise smiled enigmatically.

Shortly after the two women had left, Victor had a short visit from a Mr. and Mrs. Thompson, the parents of the little boy. They appeared to be a fairly ordinary looking young couple, although both were a little overweight, perhaps from the excesses of too much good home cooking.

"You will never know, Mr. Mallory," said Mrs. Thompson, "how sorry we are that this all happened. Little Brighton has a mind of his own, you know. If something takes his fancy, there is just no stopping him. His doctor says he has ADHD—you know, the attention deficit hyperactivity disorder—so you see, there's only so much we can do to keep him under control."

"Oh, don't worry, Mrs. Thompson. I quite understand. We had a difficult daughter at one time. Mind you, she's grown up now with a child of her own, but that must be very difficult for you if he, er, Brighton's got ADHD. And I hear you have eighteen-month-old twins as well?"

"Yes, but they're staying with their aunt at present together with Brighton. I must say it's quite nice to have a break from the kids sometimes, isn't it love?" she said, glancing at her husband.

Mr. Thompson grunted in agreement. He was definitely the quieter one of the couple and tended to let his wife do all the talking. He was indubitably quite the opposite in temperament to his hyperactive young son.

"By golly, I don't know how some parents cope these days," Victor said sympathetically.

*

By nightfall, Victor was feeling much more like his old self and was walking around the ward making light conversation with the nurses. Poor Neville on the other hand, was struggling for survival in intensive care. His family had been visiting him and keeping vigil at his bedside on an around-the-clock basis. They were fraught with worry. The visit from the Thompsons didn't seem to help matters either. In fact, they struck the distraught Yelavich family as being more of a necessary nuisance than anything.

The next morning, Victor's results came through. He was found to be extremely anemic, which helped explain why he had fainted during the horn dance. But he was still to have a follow-up test at lunchtime to see if there was any improvement.

In the meantime, the prognosis for Neville was not looking good. He had lost a lot of blood and it was looking like he might need another transfusion. Luckily, they still had plenty of his blood type available, but his internal injuries were severe. More nutrients were thus increased into his drip feed. But just as the doctors were setting up to do a second transfusion, the TV monitors delivered bad news. He was losing potassium to the extreme. His electrolyte balance was all haywire. The little beeps on the machine beside his bed then started to go crazy. There was nothing they could do. The doctor in charge called a halt and they waited in silence until the beeps finally died away. They had lost him. The Yelavich family was devastated.

*

Once the press got wind of Neville's death, the evening papers everywhere screamed the headlines, 'JESTER KILLED IN HISTORICAL HORN DANCE' all over England. Nothing like this had ever happened before in all recorded history. A Morris dancer, a mere jester, and an 'unarmed' one at that (that is, if you call carrying a coxcomb being unarmed) had been killed by one of his own kind during a re-enactment of an ancient hunting scene. It made headline news, especially now that the nine-hundred-year-old horns had been irrevocably damaged.

Victor felt terrible about it. It had been an accident and yet it had been he, Victor, who had unwittingly but ultimately been responsible for Neville's death. *After all,* he thought, *it had been his pair of antlers that had stabbed Neville to death.* Why could it not have been him who had to die? He was an old man of fifty-six and Neville had been only twenty-six. It seemed such a waste. Life could be so unfair at times. Death is so final. There would be no way of bringing Neville back now.

Louise arrived back at the hospital shortly after Victor got his last test results. He was now allowed to go home providing he took his medication to keep his hemoglobin levels stable. Needless to say, Louise was relieved at the results and glad to hear there were no other underlying more serious problems than a little innocuous anemia. However, for his own peace of mind, she encouraged Victor to visit Neville's parents as soon as he felt ready to face them. So, the next morning, Victor walked around to the Yelavichs' house on the other side of the village and knocked on the door. It was answered by the elder of Neville's two sisters, Griselda. She was twenty-three, with long, pale blonde hair and the fairest skin he had ever seen. Her green eyes peered out at him under lids puffed up from crying.

"Come in, Mr. Mallory. Father has been expecting you. Mother is indisposed."

She led him through a reception area decorated in red and black with a huge gilt mirror and umbrella stand into a huge lounge. It seemed out of proportion considering the overall size of the house itself. There were thick red velvet curtains and carpet to match, with a massive black leather lounge suite, a long antique table covered with a red table cloth, and two golden chandeliers hanging from the ceiling. Victor was impressed. He had never actually been to the Yelavichs' house before.

Mr. Yelavich entered the room, Griselda left and the two men shook hands.

"I'm so sorry about your son, Neville, Mr. Yelavich. It was a terrible accident. Terrible. If anyone had to be taken away, it should have been me."

Mr. Yelavich regarded him stonily through grief-stricken eyes. His face was pale and drawn and his skin crinkled and yellowed in places like tea-stained parchment.

"Yes, he was our only son. Our only son. Nothing can replace him. He is gone forever," he said flatly and without bitterness.

Victor felt embarrassed and guilty all at once. He coughed uneasily.

Mr. Yelavich broke the ensuing silence.

"Would you like a drink? A port, perhaps?"

"Thank you. A port would be nice."

Mr. Yelavich produced a bottle out of the antique drinks cabinet and carefully poured out two ruby ports. The overbearing silence in the room was suddenly broken again as the red liquid glugged soothingly into the crystal glasses. The thick carpet and drapes instantly swallowed up any hint of reverberation, and a certain muffled vacuousness pervaded the otherwise brittle atmosphere in the room. Mr. Yelavich handed Victor his drink.

"Thank you," said Victor.

Then to break the awkward silence again and by way of making conversation, Victor remarked, glancing sideways at his host, "I've always regretted, you know, that your Neville and our Caroline never married."

Mr. Yelavich cleared his throat. "It was never meant to be, obviously," he said hollowly.

"No," Victor agreed.

There was an embarrassing silence again. Then Mr. Yelavich said somewhat stiffly, "I don't suppose you and your team of Morris dancers would like to be pallbearers at Neville's funeral?"

Victor did a double-take.

"Of course. I would be honored. We all would."

"Good. That's settled, then."

Mr. Yelavich finished off his port and poured himself another one. "Another port?" he asked.

"Er, no, thank you," said Victor, his hand covering the top of his glass.

Mr. Yelavich took a couple of swigs of his drink and eyed Victor shrewdly.

"You don't have a son, do you, Mr. Mallory?"

"Er, no."

"No…" Mr. Yelavich reiterated slowly.

He went to the window and gazed through the net curtains with a faraway look in his eyes and then looked upon Victor again with a slight air of agitation. He fingered his glass almost nervously and then looked disconcertingly at

Victor again. He took a deep breath and then said, "We Yelavichs have a history of gypsy blood in our veins. It is very important that there is a son in the family. To carry on family tradition, you know…"

"Yes, of course," said Victor hurriedly, putting down his glass. He was starting to feel a little bit on edge.

"So, you agree to be pallbearers?"

"Yes."

"Wonderful. I will telephone you of the details in the next day or so."

He smiled disarmingly, drained the last dregs from his glass, and ushered Victor back into the entrance foyer.

"Well, thank you for your condolences, Mr. Mallory. It was nice of you to come."

He opened the front door and showed Victor out.

Victor was relieved when he had left. There was something strange about old Mr. Yelavich. It was as if he were being strangely haunted by something. But Victor supposed he had a right to be out of sorts. He had just lost his only son after all. Still, Victor was glad now that he had got that necessary little duty out of the way.

*

Neville's funeral was two days later at St Nicholas's Church. The church itself was a beautiful old Gothic structure which had been modified over the years. In the 1500s, two large windows had been cut out in the east and north walls, the roof raised and the clerestory windows added. Then after the civil war, restoration work began again in the early 1700s when the floor was leveled to emphasize that the priest and the people were now in equal status. The spire and belfry were also reconstructed and only one of the six bells still remained. In the mid-1800s, the floor was taken back to its original position once again. Originally the horns were hung in the third story of the church tower and were let down by ropes. These days however, they were housed in the side chapel, mounted on brackets set into the walls. But today of course being the day of Neville's funeral, they were out of sight, and remained conspicuously absent from the shoulders of the six deermen.

Today the whole village of Abbots Bromley was in mourning for one of its favorite sons. There was an air of shock that hung over the place. The church was decked out with lilies and white roses and the congregation was so big that it spilled out into the church grounds and onto the street.

The coffin was draped in a red velvet shroud, topped with a bouquet of red roses and Neville's red and yellow jester's cap. It was carried out of the church on the shoulders of the six deermen in their quasi-medieval costumes. The rest of the dance troupe slow marched in formation behind them to the Robinson Tune played at half speed on the accordion and triangle as they emerged through the church doors. It was a sad end for one who prided himself on being such a clever fool.

The coffin was carried to the graveside within the church grounds, where the vicar gave Neville, his final blessing surrounded by his family. He was buried between two red rose bushes at his family's request.

*

It was just days after the funeral that the press began their probing. They interviewed Victor, Louise, the Thompsons, members of the Abbots Bromley Morris Dancing Club, doctors, nurses, the TV cameramen and witnesses from the crowd on the day of the horn dance.

Victor was asked things like, 'How many times do you eat steak a week?'; 'Are you, or have you ever been, a vegetarian?'; 'What did you have for breakfast on the day of the accident?'; 'How sharp are those stag horns?'; 'How heavy are you?'; 'What made you fall?'; 'Was there ever any animosity between you and the jester?'

It was all getting to be a bit too much. Victor and his friends would be glad when everything got back to normal once more.

3

Two weeks later Victor was down at his local on a Friday night enjoying a quiet pint with his mate, Trevor. Victor was well recovered by now but missed the camaraderie of young Neville as did all the Morris men. But it was on this particular night that the rumors began. One of Neville's so-called 'mates' from the hospital in Derby was in town, standing just meters away from Trevor and Victor at the bar. Victor remembered seeing him at the funeral. He was about thirtyish, with dark, curly hair and a slight overbite. But his most prominent feature was his height or rather, lack of it, which more than accounted for his sometimes-over-pronounced voice. He was talking as if to make a big impression on the young woman he was with, a rather gullible young thing with wide blue eyes and a spiky orange-colored hairdo.

"Neville Yelavich? Oh, yeah," he said, leaning on the bar. "He was always going on about having blue blood in his veins because of his gypsy heritage. I can't think why gypsies should have blue blood though, do you?"

The girl shrugged.

"He worked with you in the blood bank, didn't he?" she asked.

"Yes. He used to drink in this bar a lot too. Did you ever see how many Bloody Marys he used to drink? He drank gallons of the stuff."

"Perhaps he was trying to go purple, you know, just to be different."

"Dunno. But with the other Morris dancer guy being found to be anemic (according to the papers), it all looks pretty fishy to me. You know what? I wouldn't be at all surprised if old Nevvy babe was a bloody modern-day vampire! A blood sucker! Did you ever notice how prominent his eye teeth were?"

"Just right for a tasty midnight snack!"

The girl, who had obviously had one too many, shrieked at her own joke and pushed the young man on the shoulder with derision. She nearly toppled off the barstool in her high heels, but was still sober enough to ask for another

37

drink. Clearly neither of them had any idea that 'the other Morris dancer guy' was sitting not more than ten feet away from them.

Victor and Trevor looked at each other blankly and shrugged. Victor drained the beer from his glass, said his goodbye to Trevor and then left. He was beginning to worry. If that's what people were saying, he was going to get to the bottom of this. *Why let others make the diagnosis?* he thought. He would make his own. He drove home through light drizzle and on the way, got himself a pizza with ham and pineapple on top. Louise would be out at a body building meeting when he got home, so he could afford to indulge himself a little.

Good, he thought. *I'll check everything out on the internet in private.*

He brewed himself a cup of coffee and took it and the pizza into his study and switched on the computer. There was nothing like a little private detective work to sort out a problem. He was totally ignorant about vampires and wanted to find out more.

He clicked onto various websites and discovered that vampires were predatory entities or demonic beings that could shape shift and become invisible. They would feed on blood, milk, sexual fluids and life forces. Victor took a bite of his pizza but was rapidly starting to lose his appetite. Gypsy vampires in particular were said to have voracious sexual appetites. Being a vampire while still alive was said to be possible if the person was a witch, a wizard, or a sorcerer.

Strange, Victor thought. *Maybe Neville was some kind of black witch perhaps. He certainly drained all the energy out of me, I know that! Cripes, every time he got near me toward the end, I felt faint!*

Becoming nervous, Victor's hands began to shake as he continued his investigation. Vampire victims, he discovered, were likely to suffer either misfortune, illness, a sapping of energy or death. Vampires were said to rise from their graves at midnight and plague their immediate family first and then the rest of the community. They would emerge from their graves if they were victims of an epidemic, if they died unrepentant of their sins, if they were improperly buried, if they were killed, murdered, or committed suicide, or if they had unfinished business with the living.

Victor cringed. He had (inadvertently admittedly) killed Neville. Perhaps Neville still had unfinished business with him. He shuddered at the thought and continued with his search. Modern day vampires wore black, silver studs, red or black fingernails, had pale faces and wore sunglasses after dark.

Oh, God! he thought. *Don't tell me Albert and Caroline are bloody vampires! They dress like that! Gothic style!*

His heart began to beat more rapidly as he read on. The text read, *Modern day vampires may sleep in coffins or use a coffin as a coffee table. They have a fondness for bats, an aversion to garlic* (he knew that) *and might wear false fangs and drink a little blood…or tomato juice as a substitute.*

That's pretty close to a Bloody Mary, if you ask me, he thought. "Vodka and tomato juice. So how do you ward off a vampire?" he asked himself, feeling slightly fearful.

He tapped the keys, clicked his mouse and came up with a few tips. Holy water, silver crucifixes, rosaries, garlic, salt, sand, tiny seeds, newspapers and mirrors.

"Mmm. Time for us to stock up, I think."

He switched to another site and found an excerpt on 'Unholy Communion'. According to John 6:53:54, Christ said, *"Whoever eats my flesh and drinks my blood has eternal life."*

This appeared to be parodying Christ's resurrection as a form of 'unholy communion' for vampires. Unimpressed, he switched to another website and found 'How to become a vampire in six easy lessons'. It began: *Take three raw egg whites, vinegar, raw chicken liver…*He immediately started to retch and switched to another website: 'The Blood Countess: Elizabeth Bathery (1560–1614)'. She was apparently a noblewoman of south east Hungary (now Romania) who upon the advice of her sorceress, Anna Darvulia, arranged to regularly bathe in fresh virgins' blood so as to retain her youthfulness.

Victor was sickened beyond belief and switched off the computer. He sat there for a moment looking at the blank screen and said to himself, "What a lot of rubbish this is. Whoever heard of modern-day vampires anyway? They're just mythological figures dreamed up by people from the Middle Ages to explain plagues and death and decay. Be sensible man, and don't worry yourself sick! This is the twenty-first century after all!"

He pulled himself together and said out loud, "I must remember that I'm a modern man at the beginning of the twenty-first century and I refuse to be intimidated by a mere myth!"

He looked at the calendar on the wall for verification. It said September 17, 2000. With that, he got up and prepared for bed. Louise would be home soon. He would leave the house lights on until she arrived home safely…

Meanwhile, a big piece of juicy ham and pineapple pizza lay forlorn and uneaten on the desk beside his computer. A big blowfly that had sneaked in the door when Victor had come home sat stealthily sucking the juice out of one of the pieces of pineapple with its proboscis pumping furiously.

4

News of the Abbots Bromley incident became national news headlines in the UK so it was not long before Caroline and Albert (Victor and Louise's daughter and son-in-law) saw the relevant footage on TV across the sea in Londonderry, Northern Ireland. Caroline promptly dispatched a 'get well' card to her father in hospital after her mother's phone call. She couldn't believe that her ex-fiancé, Neville Yelavich, could possibly have been killed by her own father. It all seemed just so incredible and coincidental. Surely it must have been an accident. A fluke in fact. Neville and her father had always been on such good terms, unlike Albert and her father.

Albert was a six-footer with shoulder length dark hair and a distinctive straight nose, combined with a rather square jawline which oddly gave him the appearance of a young Oscar Wilde. However, it was his slow speech that always put paid to that little misconception unless of course, he was trying to impress someone with a quotation from somewhere or other. Strangely enough, Caroline and Albert had been planning a trip up north to Scotland for their anniversary which was coming up on 20th September. She had mentioned to her mother on the phone that she and Albert might possibly drop in to Abbots Bromley on the way back. It was not exactly what you would call a wedding anniversary trip because it was more of an elopement that took place the previous year. (The 'hand-fasting' came later.) However, knowing the state of emotional détente that prevailed between Albert and her father, Caroline privately doubted that this little visit would ever actually take place.

"Dad would have to be on his death bed for Albert to actually make the effort," she mused. *I don't know why some families can't get on. You can pick your friends, but you can't pick your relatives or in-laws. I suppose I'm lucky in a way that Albert's parents are both dead,* she thought ruefully.

Albert was one of a pair of twins and had been left a legacy to share after his Catholic parents died during 'the troubles' in Northern Ireland some fifteen

41

years previously when the young family had lived in Belfast. The twins' mother was a political activist and lecturer at Queen's University there and their father had been a tax consultant. One morning while the twins were upstairs getting ready for school and their parents were downstairs finishing breakfast, a pipe bomb was thrown through the kitchen window. It exploded, killing their mother outright and demolishing the interior of the ground floor of the house. Their father was left in a coma for twelve weeks but never came out of it and eventually had to be taken off life-support. A Loyalist paramilitary group had claimed responsibility for the killing.

Although the twins' father had mixed heritage, the problem was that he just happened to be married to a Catholic with certain political leanings. He grew up in a Protestant area of Belfast, but in the 1960s his aunt married an IRA commandant and his father and uncles became Unionists and moved to Northern Ireland from Galway. He had always been wary of both sides.

"They're all nuts," he used to tell his boys. "I don't know what they're fighting about. It's not as if they're sitting on an oil well!" In fact, if he were ever to be accosted in the street at night by a masked man with a gun, he had a stock reply planned. "I'm Prothelic!" he would say.

That was the type of man he was; sympathetic to both sides in the polarized society that he lived in. Since 1969 more than three thousand people had died in the guerrilla war's ruthless bombings, assassinations and sectarian violence.

"You learn survival tactics," he had said to his sons. "Whenever your mother and I walk into a pub, we locate the fire exit first and never sit with our backs to the door."

He was aware that his wife had been threatened, just like some of the other Sinn Féin candidates in the area. But what he was not aware of was just how soon the threat was to be actioned. He used to tell his boys, "Suspicions are so deep here that some people believe you can actually tell the difference between a Catholic and a Protestant by sizing up the distance between a person's eyes! But don't you believe that for a second," he would say in typical Irish fashion and with a twinkle in his eye. "It's the distance between the ears that counts!"

Of course, the roots of the conflict went back to the late 1100s when Henry II sent troops over from England to subdue the Irish chieftains. Irish nationalism identified itself with the Catholic minority. Protestants who in 2000 only just commanded a slim majority of Northern Ireland's population wanted to remain part of the UK.

Loyalist paramilitary groups had sworn allegiance to Great Britain and fought to protect their Protestant traditions. They specialized in murders of political activists, random drive-by shootings of Catholics and fire-bombings. Some critics compared them to the Ku Klux Klan.

On the other hand, IRA volunteers viewed themselves as freedom fighters who wanted to expel the British. Others called them terrorists. The IRA specialized in bombings of government and commercial buildings as well as shootings of police officers, British soldiers and Protestant vigilantes. In the previous two decades, a number of IRA bombs had also killed and injured innocent bystanders.

Since the precarious peace of the 1998 Good Friday Agreement, Albert's father-in-law, Victor, had devised an amateur plan as a rank outsider to solve all the muckraking in Northern Ireland. Not that he ever discussed the matter with Albert, of course—that would be far too radical! But since his daughter, Caroline, was now living at the edge of Northern Ireland in Londonderry, he would often discuss matters with his wife, Louise in some detail. He would pontificate to her by saying, "No daughter of mine is going to live in Northern Ireland and breed a bunch of religious zealots who keep prolonging a stupid feud."

"But they're not Catholics Victor, remember? Albert and his brother became lapsed Catholics once they shifted out of Belfast to live with their Protestant uncle in Londonderry. Then later Albert became a pagan. I don't know about his brother."

"Never mind. I reckon what they need for lasting peace over there are just four things: One, withdrawal of British troops. Two, no more money to be sent to the IRA from the USA. Three, protestant annual victory marches to be abolished. Four, integration between Catholics and Protestants in primary schools. That's my humble opinion, anyway. Can you imagine what those poor little kids had to go through, running that gauntlet of hatred to that school near Belfast that time? It must have been terrible! Thank God Caroline doesn't live *there*. I just wish she and Albert would move out of Northern Ireland altogether."

"Maybe they will, Victor. Maybe they will. Albert's brother lives not too far away in the Republic of Ireland—Letterkenny, isn't it? —so maybe Albert and Caroline will move close to him some day. We'll just have to hope. I know jobs are scarce in Northern Ireland, so it's no wonder Albert lives on the dole.

Unemployment there is supposed to be the highest in Western Europe, isn't it? Perhaps one day he will see sense if he's going to support his family properly."

"Yes, let's hope so."

Albert, although a bit of a dreamer, was trying in his own spasmodic sort of way to support his wife and six-month-old son, but was tending to rely more on his inheritance at present until he found his feet in the real world. He was what you would call a late developer in the business world and spoke in a rather slow and deliberate manner which some felt made him come across as somewhat moronic. However, the opposite was in fact the case. He was an avid reader of 'catholic' tastes and was full of potential and untapped talent. It was not by chance that he had managed to sweep young Caroline off her feet in Dublin that fateful Bloomsday on June 16th the previous year when she was engaged to Neville Yelavich. He did have a certain aura and thespian charm about him when dressed in the old-fashioned garb of Leopold Bloom from James Joyce's *Ulysses*. The striped waistcoat, straw boater and round spectacles had acted like a magnet to his Molly Bloom, who had materialized before him that day as Caroline. So, he must have out-Bloomed all the other Bloomophiles present to have been able to attract her attention.

Caroline herself had blossomed into a fine and responsible young woman since the birth of young Dudley. She had recently shed six pounds, although she was still a little on the chubby side in her own opinion. She had always battled with her weight, even as a nude model, but this time she felt she deserved a reward for her pains, and what better way to celebrate than by spending their anniversary visiting the Isle of Mull in Scotland?

She had sentimental connections with the Isle of Mull because it was there that her paternal great-grandfather used to crew on one of the big paddle steamers in Victorian times. They used to ship three hundred passengers a day from there to the Isle of Staffa to see Fingal's Cave, which was a tourist attraction even back in those days. They had been known to have carried such notable passengers as Sir Walter Scott, Boswell, Dr Johnson and even Queen Victoria herself. Mendelssohn of course, wrote the famous overture 'the Hebrides', inspired by the sheer awe of this great 'cathedral of the sea'.

But it was her great-grandfather who intrigued Caroline the most. Being a Scotsman, he would ferry small groups of passengers in a small boat into the interior of the cave and then, standing amidships, would strike up on his bagpipes. The acoustics were phenomenal and so the name of Fergus Mallory, as ship's piper, went down in history among the Mallory clan.

Caroline would have liked to have made the trip the previous year, but when she fell pregnant in July, they had decided to postpone the visit due to the rather delicate state of her health. In the meantime, Caroline had left little Dudley in the trusted care of her best friend and neighbor, Davinia Trimble, whom she had known since she was six back in Abbots Bromley. Davinia was a happy-go-lucky plumpish person with freckles and brown hair and an appealing empathetic streak. By chance, she was now living near to Caroline and Albert in Londonderry, albeit as a solo mum. In fact, Davinia was such a good mother to her own little Liam that she had now become Dudley's godmother as well. Caroline and she would often babysit on a reciprocal basis, so there could not have been a more convenient arrangement.

So it was that Dudley was cared for by Davinia while Albert and Caroline went off on holiday together. They crossed the North Channel to Cairnryan on the vehicular ferry and then drove the one hundred and eighty kilometers to Oban up the scenic west coast of Scotland. Here they safely parked the car and took the ferry to the Isle of Mull. From there, they boarded a four-wheel-drive as passengers over to the western coast of the island and then boarded the tourist boat from a place called Ulva Ferry on Mull to Fingal's Cave on the Isle of Staffa.

The tourist boat carried about twenty-five passengers and after about two hours' morning sailing, they arrived at the Isle of Staffa. Staffa rose eerily out of the sea like an enormous table supported by numerous grayish-black basalt columns covered by a tablecloth of stones peppered with green and yellow lichen. As Fingal's Cave beneath loomed nearer, the skipper broadcasted an excerpt from Mendelssohn's overture over the sound system. On the front deck, Caroline stood in awe of the huge cavern and the music transported her back to the time of her great-grandfather. Albert and Caroline, together with the other passengers, were all dwarfed by this giant Scottish 'Rock of Gibraltar'. It towered one hundred and forty feet out of the sea, emphasizing their puny human insignificance.

"I would love to hear someone play the bagpipes in there," remarked Caroline. "Don't tell the skipper that. He'll think you're a real philistine," said Albert.

"But he's Scottish, isn't he?"

"Yes, but Mendelssohn was English."

"Oh."

They were soon let off the boat at a little jetty on the eastern side of the island called Clamshell Cave. Here, they climbed the aluminum and concrete stairway to the grassy flat top of the island to have lunch. About half of the traveling party then decided to trek the three hundred meters around the southern tip, down the mass of giant stepping stones to Fingal's Cave. Caroline and Albert were among the last to make the move.

At the bottom of the cliff, they entered the cave past a narrow ledge of columns leading into the darkness. Several people squeezed past them on their way out, causing them to backtrack and let them pass. One false move and they could find themselves squirming in the great cauldron of bubbling water below.

They clung to the handrail to guide them in and were amazed to see an almost perfect arched roof rising one hundred feet above the lava pillars. It was a natural cathedral, a honeycombed cavern lined with fluted columns. At the far end of the two-hundred-and-thirty-foot vestibule was a kind of natural throne, which Caroline imagined was imposing enough to seat King Neptune himself. She clung to Albert and then turned around and pointed back through the mouth of the cave. Something had caught her attention. It was the island of Iona that sat glowing like an emerald on a glistening sea in the distance. It was magical.

Unearthly sounds filled the rear of the cave and echoed around the walls with the lapping of the waves. Fascinated, Caroline strained her eyes in the semi-darkness to try to fathom how such guttural noises could be made by mere water and rock alone. Perhaps it was the voice of the Irish giant, Fingal, himself?

Suddenly, Caroline stopped dead in her tracks. She gripped Albert's arm as the voice spoke.

"Caroline," it said, "take heed of your dreams."

Caroline couldn't believe her ears. Was that really the voice of Fingal? Or was it the voice of her great-grandfather, who had been buried at sea (so the story went). Perhaps even in this very cave? It was an ancient voice, perforated by the sounds of the waves breaking on the rocks and of trapped air being compressed and decompressed in the numerous small caverns. There was no reaction from Albert, so she assumed that only she could hear the voice. She paused, straining to hear. There it was again.

"Caroline, take heed of your dreams."

And once again, only louder. "Caroline, take heed of your dreams."

Then it faded away and that was it. Just three messages and the voice was gone. Caroline shuddered. There was just the sound of the waves on the rocks now, although she strained her ears to hear more.

How strange, she thought. *But then this whole place is kind of eerie and strange.*

There was a certain timelessness about this place. It was as if she could have stayed forever. Then she felt a tug on her sleeve. It was Albert. It was time to go.

Gently, Albert guided her out through the mouth of the cave and into the pale sunshine. They blinked in the light and picked their way back over the many-sided stepping stones and up the stairway to the top of the island.

Feeling more like she was now back in the real-world Caroline took a few snapshots of Albert standing on top of the island and got another young couple of take snaps of the two of them together. Once they were all aboard again, the boat sped northward toward the Treshnish Isles and the island of Lunga. Here they landed by way of a pontoon mooring and were pulled ashore. Colonies of puffins kept them amused with their antics among the cliffs and they were deafened by the squawking of thousands of birds. Sailing north, they encountered the ruins of some ancient castles on the most outlying islands of the Treshnish Isles before spotting a family of seals at play on the nearby rocks. Then it was back to Mull and the mainland. As she looked back, Caroline could see the familiar slanting shape of Staffa adrift on the sea in the distance like a faraway water-ski jump. She felt almost as if she had left a piece of herself behind.

That night Caroline and Albert stayed in a quaint little guesthouse on the mainland. It was about two hundred years old and built of stone with a thatched roof and it faced out to sea. The two of them fell asleep almost at once as it had been such a long day, but then Caroline had a strange dream. She was standing at the altar (Neptune's throne, that is) in Fingal's Cave and hundreds of candles were lit around the walls. She was wearing a wedding gown threaded with strands of different colored seaweeds. Seahorses played in the water at her feet and bagpipe music filled the cavern. It was her great-grandfather, dressed in full Scottish regalia, standing in a small dingy and playing a lament. What could this mean? Then she saw her intended, the groom. It was Neville Yelavich, her ex-fiancé. What was he doing there? Neville walked, ghost-like, upon the water toward her from the cave entrance. The light behind him shone like a jewel. He stood beside her and gazed steadily into her eyes. Then he took her hand and placed a ring on her finger. It was dazzling and sparkled with brilliant rubies. She couldn't take her eyes off it and was absolutely riveted by the sight of this magnificent piece of jewelry. Then he kissed her—not on the lips as she expected—but lingeringly on the neck. He hung on like a leach, not letting go. Blood spurted from her neck in a huge plume across the water. When he finally let go, an enormous sea monster leaped out of the water to snaffle up the fountain of blood. Waves crashed thunderously onto the rocks around her and through all the spray and spume, she could see Neville leering at her through blood-stained lips.

Suddenly, she was wide awake. She screamed.

Albert woke up with a start.

"What's the matter, Carry?"

"Oh, I just had a horrible nightmare! Horrible! But it's okay. You weren't in it."

She lay uncomfortably awake for the next hour or so, tossing and turning and harking back to the voice she had heard in Fingal's Cave. "Take heed of your dreams," it had said. Was it really the ghost of her grandfather that had spoken to her? Perhaps it was a warning of some sort, either from him, Fergus the seafaring bagpiper, or maybe it was from Fingal, the Irish giant. But what did it all mean? And what was the meaning of that dreadful nightmare? And what, for goodness sake, did Neville Yelavich have to do with the price of fish?

5

Victoria sat in all her glory with one leg crossed over the other and gazed unflappably at her reflection in Louise's bedroom mirror. Victor 'en femme' gazed steadily back. She looked gorgeous. Blonde, beautifully-coiffed curls, thick black mascara, pale blue eyeshadow, rouged cheeks and pouty red lipstick. She was dressed in a black-sequined dress with a fringe around the hem, boat neckline and long fitted sleeves. Her fingernails were long and red to match her lips and her shoes were a dainty black strapless affair. Her legs were swathed in silky dark stockings with a silver sparkle that had a ripple effect when she flexed her calf muscles. Her drop earrings likewise sparkled and danced about her face as she moved.

She stood up and smoothed the dress over her lean hips. No, Victor was not going Morris dancing tonight. Instead, Victoria was going to a Beaumont Society dinner meeting. She aimed a kiss at herself in the mirror and ran her large hands over her smooth thighs. She loved the feeling of sheer stockings right next to her skin and always made a point of having a thorough leg and chest wax before going out.

"Are you nearly ready, Victor?" Louise called out from the kitchen.

"Nearly. Just doing the final touches."

He helped himself to some of Louise's Opium perfume from the dressing table and lightly sprayed his shaven chest, behind his ears and on his wrists. He sniffed the scent and lingered a little in front of the mirror. He was pleased with the total effect.

Meanwhile, Louise was in the kitchen making dinner for one. Beaumont Society dinner meetings were for the 'ladies' only and bona fide lady friends were not allowed. It was strictly for the cross-dressers, so Louise was making herself a cheese and bacon omelet while Victor would no doubt be partaking of fine fare and wine when he arrived at his dinner meeting in Stoke-on-Trent.

Around the walls of the Mallorys' lounge were photographic mementos of Louise's dancing career. There were photos of Louise as a child performing in *The Nutcracker Suite*, as a member of the corps de ballet in *Coppelia* and as the prima ballerina in *Swan Lake*. That part was her only claim to fame when she understudied somebody else, but the picture of her in the dying swan pose was her favorite.

But now taking pride of place in the living room was a vase of a dozen red roses on top of the baby grand piano, together with a trophy she had won in the Nottingham Women's Body Building Contest. She had won third prize. She was thrilled with the result but was now aiming even higher. As an ex-ballet dancer, she was well used to the physical and mental stamina required of her for achieving such feats.

Victor 'en femme' gave himself one last critical look in the mirror, picked up his handbag and coat and tottered into the living room. Louise had the TV on in the lounge, which she could see from the kitchen, so Victor turned down the sound and went in to get her opinion.

"How do I look?" he said, giving a twirl.

"Wonderful, darling. Just remember to stand up straight—like a ballet dancer. Don't slouch."

"Yes love. Er, no love. Oh, I'm wearing some of your Opium. Is that okay?"

"So, I noticed. I guess so. It's too late now…"

He kissed her on the cheek. Louise remembered then that he owed her a favor anyhow.

"Don't forget that we're going to little Dudley's 'christening' next week," she said. "Now that the kids are back from Scotland, we should make an effort. I would say they didn't have time to drop in on us. Probably couldn't wait to get back to the baby."

"Oh…must we?" he said weakly.

"Yes, we must, Victor. What a question! Both of us should go. We are his maternal grandparents after all. His only grandparents now that Albert's parents are gone. So I'm afraid there's no way out of it. Besides, I want to see my first grandchild. Don't you? He's six months old for gosh sake. If we don't see him now, we might never get to see him."

"Yes, of course, but you know I can't stand 'thingy'."

"Albert? Yes, I know. But we can always spend time exploring and sampling the home-grown whiskey over there. You wouldn't say no to that, would you?"

"Er, no."

"Right. That's settled, then. I'll check things out with the travel agent on Monday morning. Now, off you go and have a nice time."

Victor dutifully pecked his wife lightly on the cheek and strutted out of the door to his car. He got in and revved the motor. Of course, he wanted to see his first grandchild, but he had reservations about the visit because not only was he agin Albert, but Albert was now agin him. Albert was a Wiccan, a following which Victor had absolutely no time for and had no qualms about letting the fact be known to all and sundry. But somehow Albert had now got wind of his father-in-law's penchant for cross-dressing. So, the sword was double-edged, so to speak. The two men were hardly on speaking terms.

Suddenly Victor had an idea. If the visit to Ireland was compulsory, he might just take certain liberties to spite the lad.

When Victor had gone, Louise picked up Caroline's letter and re-read the invitation. Caroline was their only child. She had been quite a tearaway and a rebel as a teenager and after a short engagement to Neville Yelavich, had run off to live with Albert Pengally (her senior by ten years, who lived in Londonderry) when she was only eighteen. The invitation was to a Wiccan 'blessing' ceremony—a type of pagan 'christening' ritual run by modern-day witches involving magic and spells. Or, to be more exact, it was an invitation for Victor and Louise to join them after the ceremony as they—Victor and Louise—were not members of the 'inner circle'. Not that Louise was particularly worried about that, but she would be loath to miss the opportunity of visiting at all. They hadn't been invited to any official wedding as such, although they were invited to attend the reception of the 'hand-fasting'. However, they never made it to this event either, as Victor felt it was all a sham. Louise had been almost at the end of her tether at the time. However, she was thrilled now to think that she was going to see her very first grandchild for the first time the following week.

*

The day of their departure soon arrived and Victor and Louise drove to Manchester airport and flew across the channel to Belfast in Northern Ireland. From there, they hired a car and after much consultation of the local roadmap, arrived in Ballycastle, where they stayed a couple of days in a local motel. Here, Louise made sure that Victor got his recompense by pointing him in the direction of the Bushmills distillery—not that he needed that much encouragement. After sampling several glasses of the local whiskey there, they got changed into their glad rags and motored off to where the Organ Pipes were, beside the Giant's Causeway on the north Antrim coast of Ulster. The Organ Pipes are a unique formation of hexagonal-shaped basalt columns that are set by nature into the cliffs like the pipes of a church organ. It was the perfect place for a pagan christening. Local myth said that the giant, Finn McCool, left his footprints there as he trod along the coast across the top of Ireland to Scotland and back. Some said he was chasing a Scottish giant, others that he was visiting a giant ladylove in Scotland. Whatever the story, Fingal's Cave on the Isle of Staffa in Scotland is of exactly the same type of rock as these hexagonal ones on the Giant's Causeway.

Victor and Louise arrived at the Organ Pipes at the appointed time and stopped the car near an old Celtic cross by the side of the road. Down on the beach below the cliff at the water's edge, a small group of individuals dressed all in black stood around a small fire in a circle. They were witches. The Mallorys' grandson lay swaddled near the center of the circle next to the fire. Louise had the urge to rush down and scoop up the child but instead, with much self-restraint, she anxiously watched and waited. In due course, after much chanting and laying on of hands, the barefoot figures, all carrying candles, climbed up the rocky hexagonal steps in single file, Caroline straggling behind at the end of the line cradling the baby.

When she reached the top of the cliff, their eyes met and mother and daughter embraced each other and the baby in the layby at the side of the road. There were tears in Louise's eyes and the two women laughed and cried at the same time as they hugged. Albert and Victor acknowledged each other with a couple of grunts and circled each other warily. It was a bit of a standoff because of what everyone was wearing. Louise was in a dark gray pinstriped double-breasted trouser suit and straw boater with a carnation in her button hole and chunky flat shoes. Victor, on the other hand, was wearing a dress—a light, floral summer dress in polyester viscose that wouldn't crease, with high heels, blonde wig and broad-brimmed white hat. To Albert, they looked like a couple of 'tranny grannies'. Victor didn't care what Albert thought. He didn't mind 'coming out' when he was out of home range. And besides, why should he have his dress sense dictated to by his sniveling, good-for-nothing young son-in-law?

Similarly, Caroline and Albert, together with their entourage, visually impacted upon the Mallorys. They appeared to them as pale faced ghouls, their kohled eyes and black lips and fingernails giving them the appearance of belonging more to a vampire cult than a Wiccan one, for all of Caroline's valiant attempts to be 'with it' in her tight black patent leather miniskirt and black leather jacket.

The other witches then took off for their own private pagan picnic while Caroline invited her parents back to their flat, forty-five minutes away in Londonderry. Soon, the family group was ensconced in the tiny lounge room of Caroline and Albert's flat.

The two women carried the somewhat stilted conversation while the two men sat at opposite ends of the room, trying hard to ignore each other. However, neither could resist giving the other surreptitious looks over the tops of their teacups and taking mental note of how ridiculous the other looked. Albert, with his long lank dark hair, morbidly ghoulish face, tight black stovepipe trousers, black polo-necked T-shirt, and tight black leather jacket, and Victor in his flouncy summer dress, blonde wig, full make-up and high heels. Victor sat there thinking: *'Silly bugger. Looks like he's just been to a funeral! Why doesn't he get a proper job like any other self-respecting husband and father?'*

Albert, in his turn, was thinking: *'Look at that poncy fairy sitting over there. What's he got his legs crossed like that for? Covering up his dick, I suppose!'*

He smirked and looked the other way. The tension was eased a little, however, by the playful gurgling of Dudley in his cot. But this slightly dysfunctional family gathering was only to last a couple of hours before they were interrupted by a phone call on Victor's cell phone. It was the security guard people linked to the alarm monitoring system of their home back in Abbots Bromley.

"This is an emergency," a deep voice said. "I'm afraid to say that your house has been ransacked and a fire has broken out. Luckily, the Fire Service got there in time, but we would advise you to come back and check over the property immediately."

"Oh, shit!" said Victor after he had put the phone down. "This is all we need!"

They said their hurried goodbyes, kissed the baby, and took straight off for Belfast in their hire car. Here Victor, remembering the state of his dress, slipped into a ladies' toilet at a petrol station and changed back into normal attire before sneaking back to the car when the coast was clear. They got tickets on standby back to Manchester airport and arrived in pouring rain in the middle of an unexpected thunderstorm. Brollies up, they located their car and then joined the crawling traffic out of Manchester and back to Abbots Bromley. All the way home, Louise worried about the tense relationship between her husband and son-in-law.

"But what else can you expect between a witch and a fairy?" she privately reasoned. Just as they arrived at the house, the rain stopped and an eerie yellow-green afternoon sun filtered through the clouds. The house had been cordoned off and one slightly damp security guard stood at the gate. They showed him their ID and were allowed in.

Entering the house, they were struck by the smoke-blackened interior, curtains ripped off railings, overturned furniture and belongings strewn everywhere. They didn't know where to look first. The blackest part of the house was the lounge and around the fireplace. The bedrooms had hardly been touched by the smoke, except that a lot of Louise's and Victoria's frocks had been slashed and strewn all over the floor.

Luckily, Louise's mementos on the lounge walls appeared to have been only slightly smoke-damaged, but her tutu (the one she had kept from *Swan Lake*) had been taken out of one of the wardrobes in the spare room and slung over the open keyboard of the baby grand. It sat teetering on the brink like a giant black and white puffball, as unstable as a dandelion seedhead caught up in a gentle breeze. Her ballet shoes, tied together, had been slung around the upright holding up the piano lid, and hung mournfully down from the body of the tutu like the broken neck of a dying swan. It was pure pathos. Louise's breath was taken away and she must have stood there for at least five minutes, shell-shocked, staring at what used to be her life.

She held her breath and wondered if she dare venture into the sewing room. One look was enough to confirm her fears. She called out for Victor. He entered the room and there they were confronted by the sight of her brass tailor's dummy, which had not only been blackened with soot, but also abused. It stood there in the middle of the room, kitted out in Louise's best purple patterned chiffon layered skirt, and topped with what had once been her white fringed silk handkerchief top. Victor's best evening suit jacket and bow tie had been placed over the top. The whole half-and-half outfit had been draped with the fairy lights from their Christmas decoration box and Christmas glitter sparkled on the charred shoulder pads in the eerie shafts of chartreuse-colored sunlight that sneaked through the blackened window panes. To finish off the sartorial effect, the Christmas fairy that normally sat on top of the tree had been inserted into the breast pocket of Victor's coat and had one sooty foot poking out. "Oh, my God!" groaned Victor. "Who is doing this to us?"

They waded back through the cut-up clothing and into the lounge. That was when Louise suddenly noticed that her dozen red roses were no longer in their vase. They had been scattered indiscriminately over the exposed piano strings like spilled blood. The vase and trophy, she noticed, had been smashed to smithereens against the flagstones of the fireplace.

She stared into the darkness of the fireplace. She wasn't sure, but she thought for a moment she saw something big and black with ribbed wings flapping at her in a cloud of soot. A second glance confirmed it was only a half-burned log that had fallen out of the grate and triggered a sooty cloud. But then she started to wonder…

Was there something supernatural about this break-in, or was it just her imagination? It had to be someone who knew of them somehow. But what about the fire? It wasn't as if they had lit a fire in the grate before they left, although they did tend to leave it always full of pinecones. So, was it an electrical fault, or was it arson?

She was churning it over in her mind, not knowing what to think, when suddenly another log fell with a thump out of the grate. Startled, her head swiveled in the direction of the fireplace. Then she asked out loud somewhat timorously, "Is this a hex, or just a case of witches and fairies…?"

6

Louise stood among the debris in her apron, one hand on her hip and broom in the other. With her were two young police officers searching for fingerprints. It was now a week after the fire and Louise was doing the lion's share of the final clean up before commercial cleaners arrived the next day. Victor had got off relatively lightly because of his work.

It was a thankless task. The police had searched but were unable so far to find any evidence of entry. The locks had not been tampered with, no windows or doors had been forced and there were no fingerprints anywhere. It was a total mystery. The only available open entranceway was down the chimney.

"You don't think, officer, that someone very small might have come down the chimney, do you?" Louise asked.

"I don't think so, madam. There's certainly a lot of soot about though. No footprints…It's a strange one, this…"

He scratched his head, a little perturbed. Louise looked similarly perplexed. Then one of the policemen suddenly spotted a black cat leaving sooty footprints on the path outside and realized he had left the back door open.

"Oh, that's Sooty from next door being nosy," said Louise. "She's just not stupid enough to come down a chimney, so that's let her off the hook. She's way too clean and fussy."

Even as she spoke, the cat sat down and began fastidiously cleaning its dirty paws. The two young officers finished powdering the window sills and promised they would keep the place under surveillance for the next week in case anything else suspicious cropped up. They would keep the case open, they said.

Louise served them morning tea before they left and then began packing things away into boxes. She and Victor had decided to move permanently into rental accommodation and to sell their house once it was cleaned up and repaired. *There is nothing more stressful than moving house—unless you count an accident, sickness, a fire and a break-in,* she thought. It was almost too much. It was almost as if they were jinxed.

Louise packed away box after box of clothes (or what was left of them), framed photographs and personal bits and pieces until she had packed almost as much as she could. She stood back and stared at all the memories going into the last cardboard box. Her life was being compartmentalized into boxes. Suddenly the tears welled up and she began to cry.

Why, why was all this happening to them? What had they done to deserve this, that they should now be forced to leave their beloved home? They had lived in this house for over twenty years, for gosh sake, since before Caroline was born, and now look at it! A burned out, blackened shell, smoke damaged beyond recognition. She felt the tears flow.

Suddenly, the phone rang. She dried her eyes and blew her nose. It was Victor ringing from work.

"Louise? It's me. How are you doing? Just a quick call. I've had a couple of the lads volunteer to help with the clean-up at the weekend, so we won't need the commercial cleaners after all. Hopefully, you're not feeling too overburdened there."

"No, I'm coping, thanks. But that would be great if we could get some extra help. Give them my thanks. I'll serve fresh Devonshire teas to all who lend a hand."

"In that case, we may get more!"

"The more, the merrier."

"The other thing is that one of the boys from Morris dancing, Maid Marion—you know, Humphrey Johansen—well, he's having an engagement party on Saturday night and we're invited."

"Oh, who's he getting engaged to? Young Josephine?"

"That's the one. Josephine, the bossy one."

"He must like being bossed around."

"Yes, well, I'd say she's the one who wears the pants."

"Sounds a bit like us! But I'm not that bossy, am I?"

"No, darling. You're just perfect." He cleared his throat. "So, I'll tell him we're on, shall I? It's down at the King's Arms at seven thirty on Saturday night."

"Sounds great."

"See you later then. Bye love."

"Bye."

Louise felt a little more buoyed up at this news and poured herself another cup of tea. Then suddenly she wondered what on earth she was going to wear on Saturday night. Her favorite black and white top had been cut to shreds, so she would have to wear her red outfit instead, the red jacket and skirt with the black silk camisole underneath. Yes, that would do nicely.

*

On the night, Louise looked very chic in what was left of her suddenly diminished wardrobe, and Victor wore his dark gray trousers, pastel colored shirt and houndstooth jacket. They looked quite the conventional couple.

The King's Arms was a buffet-style restaurant decorated in plush green velvet upholstered seats, wallpaper striped in green and white, with alcove dining and one large central table for large groups. Heraldic shields and coats of arms were interspersed around the walls with several stuffed stag heads, all at least sixteen-pointers, staring down glassy eyed at the diners.

Maid Marion, the guest of honor, was rather suavely dressed in a conventional suit and his fiancée was wearing trousers as well. Louise took mental note. Sitting next to Josephine, Louise was surprised to see Larry (Old Dobbin) with Elspeth, her protégé. "Hello, Elspeth! Fancy seeing you here!"

"Hello there, Louise! Larry brought me because I've been teaching him a few more new dance steps."

"Oh, you mean like the Lipizzaner horses do in Vienna? A bit much for our Ol' Dobbin, isn't it?"

"Maybe, maybe not. Four legs are always more of a challenge than two. I had to throw him in at the deep end and get him well trained with a bit of discipline from the start."

"So, when did you become a horse whisperer?" asked Victor.

"Oh, I've always had a way with animals…"

"Even two-legged ones?" asked Louise.

"Yes."

"Hey! I'm no animal," Larry piped up. "I'm a man!" he said proudly, puffing out his chest.

"Yes, but you've got lovely soft ears and big brown eyes," Elspeth said endearingly.

"Oh…oh…yes, I have, haven't I?" said Larry, stroking his earlobes appreciatively and fluttering his eyelashes at her.

"A bit like that big stag's head up there," said Elspeth, pointing over his head.

"That one's been looking at me ever since I came in," said Louise.

"It's because you're wearing red. He's a bull stag, remember, not a Bambi," said Victor.

"Oh," said Louise, somewhat deflated. Then, turning to Elspeth, she said, "Well, it's nice to see you again Elspeth…you and Larry. Have you met Humphrey and Josephine?"

"Yes, thank you."

Josephine smiled and put a protective arm around her husband-to-be. No one was going to steal her man from her, let alone on their engagement night. Whatever Josephine wanted, she usually got. She was a very determined young woman and she could be quite bolshie about things if she wanted to.

Trevor Taylor, who had been fairly quiet up until then, with eyeing Humphrey's rather conservative tie, suddenly piped up in a feigned upper-class accent, "I say, Humphrey old boy…er, Maid Marion, sorry…ever considered taking it up seriously as a hobby?"

He pulled at the knot of his own tie and shook his head from side to side as if his tie were too tight. There was a huge twinkle in his eye.

"What's that?" asked Humphrey.

"You know. Dressing up as a woman. You do it so well."

"Phouaw! What do you take me for? I'm just an amateur doing it for fun. You know that! Besides, I've got a real woman right beside me now, haven't I Jose?"

"Yes. And Humphrey's a real man," retorted Josephine rather too vehemently. "He's no ponce. I should know. Men who dress up as women to get their kicks are perverts. They shouldn't be allowed out."

"Just joking. Just joking," said Trevor, with one hand up as a sign of pacification. Victor looked blankly at Josephine, and then looked the other way.

"Some women!" he fumed silently to himself. "They certainly do take the cake! They wear trousers, so why shouldn't men wear skirts if they want? My grandfather wore a kilt and even the ancient Greek army wore thigh-high little pleated numbers. What about the Roman gladiators and the ancient Egyptians?

Silly cow! She's just a bigot. Obviously, she never saw that wonderful drag queen as Mrs. Coleman (or was it Goldman?) in *The Birdcage*. So maternal and womanly, even though a bit ditzy. Even the Senator for Moral Values in the film loved her!

He began to whistle silently to himself as he gazed nonchalantly around the room. His little reverie was interrupted, however, when Louise nudged him for another top up of her wineglass. "Where are you, Victor? Away with the fairies?" she said to him in a loud whisper.

"Yes, as a matter of fact, I am."

"Well, just a little top up, thanks, love. No need to blow a gasket."

Victor leaned forward and did the honors.

*

Counting heads, there would have been a good forty people at the table that night, most of whom were Morris dancers. Apart from that one little incident cropping up, the evening proved a much-needed light relief for Victor and Louise. Toward the end of the evening and after much merriment, Humphrey remarked to Louise, "Sorry to hear about your fire and break-in Louise."

"Yes, Victor and I were horrified. We're still not over it, are we Victor?" she said, turning toward Victor, who was listening patiently to Josephine prattle on about her wonderful Humphrey.

"Er, pardon dear? No, dear."

"Well, never fear you two," said Humphrey magnanimously. "Robin Hood and his Merry Men will protect you, and we'll help with the clean up again tomorrow, won't we lads?"

He repeated himself above the din and stood up with his glass held high and rocked back and forth on his heels. Everyone at the table then raised their glass and Humphrey made a toast.

"To Victor and Louise. May Robin Hood and his Merry Men help and protect them!"

"To Victor and Louise. May Robin Hood and his Merry Men help and protect them!" everyone chanted in unison.

Victor was touched, so stood up and replied to the toast.

"Thank you everyone. Thank you. And now a toast to the happy couple on their engagement. To Humphrey and Josephine!"

"To Humphrey and Josephine!" everyone chanted, and drank to their health. All except Robin Hood, it seemed… The young Gabriel Taylor who had just turned sixteen the day before. Suddenly, someone realized he was missing.

"Hey! Where's Robin Hood, our great protector?"

"Can't handle his grog. He's out in the men's room having a chunder…"

7

In mid-January, Albert went away for around ten days with his twin brother, Edwin, and some of his old school mates to watch a rugby union tournament at the indoor stadium in Wales, leaving Caroline at home with Dudley in Londonderry. Seeing that she had the whole week virtually to herself, Caroline decided that it was the perfect opportunity to knuckle down and lose the remaining puppy fat that she had gained while she had been pregnant. She had been feeling a bit frumpy since the birth back in April last year and decided to surprise Albert with a new look when he got back. She would never pose nude the way she looked now—not even for her husband.

She glanced at the calendar on the kitchen wall to check that she would have enough time to do this and happened to notice that St Agnes Day was coming up shortly on 22nd January. *That must be the same St Agnes Day as in Keats's poem,* she thought. She had seen the poem in an old volume of poetry that Albert had inherited from his father and she decided to re-read it. She reached over to the bookcase in the lounge, found the book and flicked through the musty pages until she came to the narrative poem called *The Eve of St Agnes.* It read:

They told her how, upon St Agnes Eve
Young virgins might have visions of delight
And soft adorings from their loves receive
Upon honey'd middle of the night
If ceremonies due, they did aright
As supperless to bed they must retire
And couch supine their beauties lily white
Nor look behind nor sideways but require
Of Heaven with upward eyes for all that they desire.

The legend really only applied to young unmarried girls, but Caroline didn't mind. She was ready to give anything a go if it helped her to lose those extra few final pounds.

"Perhaps I should aim on St Agnes Eve to go supperless to bed, just like in the legend," she mused. *It all acts as extra incentive to go on a diet and especially if some lover comes to my bedside while Albert's away,* she thought impishly. *I might give it a try.*

Feeling thus inspired, she resolved to go on a crash diet of herbal teas and grapefruit juice—a liquid diet. She would start tomorrow and maybe cast a few spells to hurry things along. In the meantime, she might just finish off that cinnamon bun with the coconut icing in the pantry and maybe even scrape that hokey pokey ice cream carton clean. She hated seeing things left to go off. Such a waste.

She went to the kitchen, got butter out of the fridge, spread it on the bun (thickly) and stood leaning against the bench munching it appreciatively until it was gone. Then she did the same with the ice cream. There, that was better. The pantry and the freezer looked a whole lot tidier now. Yes, she decided she would start the diet tomorrow with a clean slate.

Feeling replete, she wandered back into the lounge and absent-mindedly picked up Albert's black mirror that he had left lying on the coffee table. Being a 'black' mirror, it was without a mirrored surface, so she could see no reflection of herself in it. He used this for scrying into the future as a divining device, a bit like gazing into a crystal ball. As a fairly well-versed Wiccan, he had quite a few pieces of paraphernalia in his collection that he normally kept tucked away in his study. Caroline turned the mirror over and over in her hands and wished that she could get the thing to work as well for her as it did for him. Then on an impulse, she decided to have another go with it. She drew the curtains to dim the morning light and turned on a tape of soft Enya music. Dudley was having a nap so she reckoned on being uninterrupted for a while. She carefully placed the oval black mirror on the coffee table and stared intently into it.

"Concentrate…meditate…visualize…" she told herself. She knelt in front of the mirror in a trance, willing herself to see things in its surface. After about ten minutes of concentrated effort, she was surprised to see a cloudiness in front of the mirror. Then it cleared and she could vaguely make out moving shapes. She was elated. It was finally working for her! She sat entranced and watched in gradual recognition of the central figure. It was a picture like a hologram of her husband and surrounding him were dancing figures. She peered at them more closely and realized that these dancing figures in actual fact had wings. They were fairies! Her husband was at the center of a fairy ring! But that didn't make sense.

"That's ludicrous!" she cried. "Albert hates fairies—all kinds!"

Immediately, the vision was snuffed out. Caroline sat staring at the black mirror in disbelief. She got up, a little miffed with this revelation and resolved to not let it be known to Albert. Besides, he would not believe such a situation possible. After all, who were the most powerful—witches or fairies? She knew what Albert would say to that all right!

She sighed and went back to the kitchen to see if anything else needed 'tidying up'. Perhaps she had missed something…

*

The next morning, Caroline was up bright and early and got stuck into her chamomile tea and grapefruit drink. She consulted Albert's *Book of Shadows* containing various spells and found one that was designed to make you lose weight. She needed several special ingredients: a seven-day black candle (to banish the weight), a piece of black onyx, some lemon balm essence, yarrow, juniper berries, cypress, and mistletoe as a catalyst. These she found in Albert's private pantry, which he kept in his study. She followed the instructions, which said to place all these ingredients around the candle on a small ceramic dish inside a glass jar. Then she lit the candle and visualized herself as being extremely thin, but not anorexically thin. Once this was done, she placed the whole concoction in the bathroom to burn happily away for the next seven days. The moon was in its waning phase, so that augured well for even better results. By the time St Agnes Eve had arrived, Caroline had lost three pounds. She was thrilled. All she had to do now was stick to the chamomile tea and grapefruit juice and prepare herself meticulously for bed that night.

"You never know who might come to my bed tonight," she giggled to herself.

That evening, when Dudley was safely tucked up in his cot, Caroline bathed in a warm bath infused with twelve drops of rose oil and dressed herself in her best silk nightie. She cast another spell from Albert's book, this time with a pink candle (for romance), and amethyst, rose oil, three special herbs, and mistletoe. She drank a toast to St Agnes of purified water from Albert's chalice, played a tape of soft Celtic harp music, and went 'supperless to bed'. That night she wanted to dream 'the dream of the goddess'. She was soon fast asleep.

By midnight, Caroline was sleeping peacefully in her bed. The net curtain in the open window of her upstairs bedroom fluttered slightly in the light breeze that had just now sprung up. A faint glimmer of moonlight from the waning moon lit up the windowsill.

The clock downstairs in the hall struck twelve and Caroline stirred. There was a rustling of curtains as something alighted upon the windowsill. It shuffled forward and sat like a vulture; its wings folded. It licked its lips. It had long spiked clawed fingernails and fangs.

It alighted beside her bed and gently pierced her white neck with its needle-like fangs and began to suck. Her lifeforce was being weakened while its own lifeforce was being strengthened. Caroline became semi-paralyzed in her comatose state and the thing began to undress her. It knew that she would be available for more over the next two nights.

Caroline was dreaming of a lover coming to her on St Agnes Eve. He was caressing her breasts as if wanting to suckle her milk, but it had all dried up. He pulled the bedclothes off and then pulled off her nightdress more urgently. He appeared invisible except to Caroline in her dream. He salivated, hovering above her naked body, his eyes glowing like hot coals.

Suddenly, Caroline awoke and snatched at the bedclothes. Her face contorted and she shivered uncontrollably. She had recognized her ex-lover in an altered form. She screamed and he balked. She starting throwing anything she could lay her hands on—bedside clock, perfume, pillow—straight at him, but everything went right through him. Suddenly she felt revitalized. Perhaps it was just the sheer horror of recognition.

"Get away! Get away, you beast!" she yelled shrilly.

Neville drew himself up to his full height, took in a deep breath and wrapped his black cloak around him.

"Very well, my dear. You taste very nice tonight, but I shall give you a reprieve. But I warn you, I shall have you. Never fear—I will return."

With that, he hopped nimbly onto the windowsill and flew off, his cape fluttering brazenly between his legs as he went and his two pet bats following behind.

Caroline was hyperventilating in horror. That was her ex-boyfriend, Neville Yelavich, the one she nearly married! She couldn't believe her eyes! Still the gentleman as always, even in vampire form, she noticed. So, what went wrong with her special spell for *him* to be attracted to her on St Agnes Eve? Of all people, why did it have to be him?

She clutched the bedclothes to her breast and shivered.

Trust Albert to be at a footie match in Wales just when I need him! she thought. *I can't even get in touch with him because he doesn't have a cell phone and I don't know how to contact his mate Callum either!*

Suddenly, she was horror-struck. "What about poor little Dudley?"

She scrambled into her nightdress and dressing gown and ran desperately into the next room. She was relieved beyond belief. There he was, sleeping peacefully, blissfully unaware of any goings-on in the main bedroom.

"Thank God for that!" Caroline blurted out. "If that Neville creature had laid one finger on him…!"

She paced around the house for the next hour or so, drinking cups of tea fitfully before falling asleep exhausted on the couch downstairs. She awoke late the next morning to the sound of Dudley crying for a feed, and dragged herself up to face the day. How was she going to cope? She knew that Neville was coming back, perhaps even that very night.

She rummaged through some of the books in Albert's mini-library for help and soon discovered what she would need to do. She must make a trip to a furniture store that day, to the grocer, the greengrocer, and the newsagent. She readied Dudley for an outing in the pushchair later that morning and purchased the required articles. Then she telephoned for an odd job man to install the large mirror she had just bought at the head of the bed in the main bedroom, so now there would be a large mirror both at the head of the bed as well as the original one at the foot on the wall opposite.

"You sure you've got enough mirrors in here, ma'am?" asked the odd job man. "I can fit a ceiling one as well if you want. No job too big or small," he grinned.

"No, that will be fine, thank you, Mr. Malone. Just the one extra for now."

Mr. Malone seemed a bit disappointed, especially as she knew what was going on in his little mind. He could enhance this young couple's love life for just a few more measly Irish pounds from out of their hard-earned savings.

"Well, don't say I didn't offer," he said salaciously.

Caroline smiled sweetly and readily paid the man cash just to get rid of him.

"He was a slimy character if ever there was one," she thought. *I definitely won't be recommending him to Davinia.*

As soon as he was out of the door, Caroline grabbed her bag of groceries and sprinkled poppy seeds all around the bed in the master bedroom. Then she hung bunches of garlic over the four bedposts as an extra safeguard and from the newsagent's shopping bag, she spread oodles of different newspaper publications all around the room.

This done, she waited with bated breath until nightfall. The stress of it all had left her feeling a little out of sorts all day. She had been uncharacteristically impatient with Dudley and deliberately overfed him before she put him to bed early.

That night, she lay in bed with one eye constantly open until midnight, half excited and half petrified. At midnight as expected, there was a light tapping and a black shape appeared at her bedroom window. It was Neville's alter ego, the vampire. He hovered menacingly over Caroline's bed, wringing his clawed hands and salivating expectantly. His eyes radiated with hot passion.

"Why do you do it, Caroline?" he demanded evenly.

"Do what?" she squeaked in a strangled voice.

"Go on crash diets. They don't make any difference to me. You still taste the same. You are just as ripe and juicy. In fact, when you're dehydrated, the taste is more concentrated. So, on second thoughts, stop the diet."

"Mind your own bloody business! I was dieting for Albert and me and my St Agnes Eve dream lover!"

"That was me!"

"No, it wasn't. Don't make me laugh. You are a nightmare lover!"

"Why, you little…"

"You never were any good, Neville."

She was feeling extra bold with all her anti-vampire devices around her.

"Here, have a poppy seed or read the news! Make yourself at home," she said challengingly.

"Bloody Mary! You've really done your homework, haven't you? I suppose it's all that newfound Wiccan knowledge that you get from that numbskull husband of yours!"

"Yes, that's right. He may look like a numbskull to you, but at least he has learned from the 'olde ways' to do good. He's a white witch, remember, not a black one like you seem to have become. Why did you do it?"

"Do what?"

"Become a vampire."

"It runs in the family. We have a history of vampirism in the eldest male of every family group going back nearly one thousand five hundred years to our roots as gypsies from Moldavia. Of course, we have evolved since then and become much more considerate of our victims. Notice that I didn't ravish you last night?"

"Yes, I did notice that. Very polite. You've come a long way in one thousand five hundred years."

She paused and licked her lips nervously, looking around while he stood on tip-toe, about to pounce and trying to catch her off-guard. She propped herself up on her pillow.

"Now don't forget that before you can pounce, you have to pick up each of those poppy seeds one by one and read that pile of newspapers to me out loud. By the time you've done that, it should be morning. And remember, you're allergic to sunlight, so you'll have to leave early."

Neville was not used to bossy women, even if he *did* have two younger sisters himself. Why did this woman, his intended victim have to be such bossy britches? He decided to swallow his pride and do what he must, so he obediently bent over at the foot of the bed and began to pick up the poppy seeds one by one.

"And while you're at it," she called, "don't forget to look over here to see if there's someone else in the room!"

She pointed to where she estimated his reflection might be in the mirror behind her. He looked up. He had been tricked. To his horror, he saw an infinite number of her reflections in the two mirrors in front of and behind her and an infinite number of invisible reflections of himself. He had been indefinitely stalled and immobilized. Damn! The only way for him to escape now before sunrise would be if he could physically be moved from the spot he was in or if one of the mirrors themselves was physically removed.

"Help!" he cried weakly, like a wolf in sheep's clothing.

"Don't give me that, Neville. It's your own fault. You shouldn't have come back."

"But I love you!" he cried.

"What?"

"I'm sorry and I promise I won't do it again. Just set me free, will you? I don't want to die," he whimpered. "I want to be immortal and live forever and ever and sleep in my coffin every day along with my grandfather, great-grandfather and all the others in Moldavia. It's our own little gentlemen's club and we all go out together at midnight, do our thing, and then go home and tell of our exploits over a few Bloody Marys. I don't want to give all that up…plus my eternal youth, you know."

"Eternal youth?"

"Yes. I'll always be twenty-six, no matter how long I live."

"Well, I wouldn't want to begrudge you that. Frankly, though, I'd rather be alive and young than dead and young."

"But I'm not dead, Caroline. I'm one of the undead."

"Oh, sorry…"

"Well, are you going to help me get out of this mess or not?"

"Okay…but only if you promise never to come back. I just don't want to see you again. Not like this."

"All right. It's a deal. I won't come back."

She got up, went to him and they shook hands, his damp, cold, clammy grasp in hers. Then with much effort, she pushed his rigid body, which had materialized under the spell of the mirrors, toward the corner of the bed. He immediately began to dematerialize and breathed a sigh of relief.

"Thank you, Caroline," he said. "You have saved my life."

"You're welcome," she said. "But remember, just don't come back."

"I won't."

Then doggedly, he bent down and resumed picking up the poppy seeds one by one with his spindly fingernails until they were all in a neat little pile beside her bed. And luckily for him, he was a speed reader, so he was able to get through all the newspapers relatively quickly, especially as Caroline relented and let him off having to read out loud. When he had finished, it was still before dawn and so they shook hands again and he left before sunrise.

By this time, Caroline was feeling rather tired. However, she was feeling a whole lot less tense about things now, and much less on edge. She had won that round all right and she was pretty sure she could trust Neville. After all, he was an old friend, she had saved his life and he had given his word that he would not come back.

*

She was woken at 7 am when Dudley wanted his bottle, and so she spent the morning endlessly fussing over him. Now that Albert was away and not there to play with him, Dudley had become more demanding of Caroline's time. Not that she minded. He was a sweet little fellow…most of the time. But no matter how hard she tried; she couldn't get the events of last night out of her mind. "Vampires?" she asked herself. "Ghosts, yes, but vampires? I can't believe it. It must have all been a dream. A nightmare follow up of St Agnes Eve's dream of the goddess."

Just to make sure, she went upstairs again to check in the bedroom. Sure enough, there was a little pile of poppy seeds in the corner beside her bed and there was a stack of neatly folded newspapers sitting at the side of her bed.

"So, it's true! Neville really did visit me last night. And I beat him at his own game, look at that! Just wait till I tell Albert!"

Albert was due home the next morning at the latest, so Caroline decided to take Dudley down to the local shops to buy a roast of beef for tomorrow night's dinner. Albert was no vegetarian, he was a real he-man carnivore, just like her father, Victor.

Funny that, she thought. *These two are so different in some ways and yet exactly the same in others.*

She put on a little lipstick and touched up her finger and toenails with her favorite bright red nail polish and bundled Dudley into his pushchair. She would spoil herself tonight as well, with half a dozen oysters in preparation for Albert's return. A little aphrodisiac in advance would not go astray, as his mother always used to say.

"A little bit of zinc keeps you in the pink," were her exact words, according to Albert, so Caroline recalled. She had never forgotten that little piece of advice of her mother-in-law's. If Albert ever complained that she had been spending too much money lately, she would just tell him that his very own mother had always recommended oysters as a pick-me-up. That was usually sufficient to keep him quiet.

So, at dinner time that night Dudley had his usual baby food slop and Caroline had oysters au naturel, followed by steamed fish and veggies. There was nothing remotely interesting on TV that night, so once Dudley was in bed, Caroline retired early.

However, by 10.30, she was beginning to get stomach cramps. She lay there for some time, tossing and turning from side to side, before finally getting up to soothe her stomach with some chamomile tea. However, this still didn't give the instant relief she needed, so she ran a hot bath as well. She turned on the hot tap and wondered whether it was the oysters that had done this to her but they hadn't smelled suspicious at the time. It was very strange. Perhaps they really had been 'off' and she hadn't realized.

Into the bathwater she poured some essential oils—rather too much in her semi-somnambulant state, but the aroma was pure heaven. She lit a candle, took off her robe and climbed in, luxuriating in the soporific vapors. She was thankful for the inheritance that Albert had received from his parents because they were able to afford such little luxuries. Her stomach cramps eased slowly away and by midnight she had fallen asleep in the candlelight to the gentle lapping of the waves upon her body.

She was dreaming. The pain had almost gone now and she could feel a light tickling on her skin. She quivered. Warm water began to trickle down her neck and between her breasts. It was very erotic—orgasmic, even. She shifted her weight a little in the bath and moaned slightly. Had her dream lover arrived at last? Through the veil of her closed eyelids two eyes glowered at her like hot coals. A pair of huge black-cloaked arms folded themselves around her as if she were a tiny sparrow about to be crushed by a vulture.

Suddenly she was wide awake. A paroxysm of flailing black sleeves and naked white limbs began splashing chaotically in the bathwater. It was a real feeding frenzy. Grotesque dark shadows of wickedly long fingernails spidered fleetingly across the ceiling. The candle flame buffeted bravely under the onslaught and big gobs of flying soapsuds splatted onto the mirror, obliterating any possible image of the perpetrator. Deep guttural utterances, hungry for blood, could be heard between stifled screams. The bathwater slowly turned red. She was not being molested, but murd…

"Arrrghhh!" she cried.

The splashing grew more spasmodic as she succumbed to the inevitable. Soon there was silence. Nothing stirred. The water lay mirror-still. The life had been sucked out of her.

*

The next morning, there was a click as a key turned in the front door lock. It was Albert. He was loaded down with a duffel bag full of dirty washing and looked a little unkempt. Ten days away with the lads, you see…He was met by the sound of crying. It was Dudley.

"Caroline? Caroline? Are you there?"

There was no immediate answer, so he ran upstairs to Dudley's room. Dudley was in his cot, drenched in a dirty nappy and cold and hungry.

"Shit! Where are you, Caroline? Caroline?" he called.

Again, there was no answer. He dithered, not knowing exactly what to do before picking up Dudley (which quietened him a little), and wandering aimlessly from room to room looking for Caroline. Dudley smelled terrible but first things first. He looked in the main bedroom, but she wasn't there—only a new mirror and a pile of newspapers, from what he could see. Also, some strings of garlic on the bedposts, he noted.

"Strange. Let's check the bathroom, Dudley."

He pushed open the bathroom door. Dudley whimpered. There, to his horror was Caroline in the bath, deathly pale and surrounded by a pool of blood-stained water. She was very still and there was a bright red wound upon her neck.

"Oh my God!" said Albert.

He gently put Dudley on the floor and bent over to feel his wife's forehead.

"Cold! Oh my God!"

He felt for her pulse. Nothing.

"Oh no! She's dead!"

He suddenly felt faint and had to sit down. He put the toilet seat lid down and sat on it with his head between his hands. He sat for some moments before daring to peek out between the cracks in his fingers to see if it was really true.

She looked so slim and beautiful…so unbelievably slim…and her fingernails and toenails looked so startingly red against her deathly white skin…

8

When Victor and Louise in Abbots Bromley were notified by the police of Caroline's death, they were stunned. It just didn't seem possible that someone who was so full of life could suddenly be snuffed out like that. It just didn't seem real. Caroline was their only child and only just out of her teens.

They immediately departed for Ireland from Manchester airport and descended upon Albert and Dudley in Londonderry by rental car. Albert himself was at a complete loss and seemed peculiarly quite glad of his in-laws' support, especially now as there were still detectives in the house. He was utterly hopeless in the kitchen, so appreciated Louise being around in spite of the fact that she would keep bursting into tears at the most unpredictable times. By Victor's presence however, he was less impressed. However, under the circumstances the two men managed somehow to co-exist peaceably enough under the same roof. Any dialogue between the two of them seemed to be made through Louise as mediator. Little Dudley of course was the center of attention and the apple of his grandparents' eyes. He could do no wrong and acted as a buffer for all the emotional upset in the house.

"Let me change Dudley for you, Albert. There's no need for you to do it while I'm here," Louise would say.

Albert would reply rather stoically, "But I'm a solo father now. I've got to learn some time."

"Okay, let me show you the proper way to change a nappy…"

She would then take over, roll up her sleeves, fill her mouth with safety pins and get to it. Albert would learn from Louise's expertise and then have a go himself.

"That's the stuff. You've got the hang of it now. Show Victor your handiwork."

Albert would then hold up Dudley for Victor to see, and Victor would say, "Mmm…very neat."

So that was praise indeed coming from him. Albert would make his in-laws endless cups of tea and they would talk about Caroline's short life and the type of funeral she might want.

"Caroline would want a Wiccan funeral," Albert said to Louise. "I'm sure of that. She really became very interested in the craft recently and had been coming to some of our circles."

"But…" Victor would say, slightly alarmed for his daughter.

"Hush, dear," Louise would butt in, glancing disapprovingly at him. "Albert's right, Victor. Caroline was his wife and as such, it is his decision as to the type of funeral that she has. As long as we are there, that's all that counts."

"I never knew Caroline had taken it up that seriously," said Victor helplessly to Louise.

"You never asked," said Louise.

"Mmm…" said Victor, looking pensive.

"So, I thought we might have the funeral service in the little chapel out toward Malin Head on the Inishowen Peninsula. Then we could have her cremated and I could scatter her ashes out to sea," said Albert looking at Louise for confirmation.

Unannounced, Louise immediately began to cry and dabbed her eyes delicately with her handkerchief.

"I can't believe that our Caroline's gone. She was so full of life only a few months back when we were here for Dudley's christening. She had so many plans for Dudley and was a wonderful natural mother. I don't know how I shall cope without her being around," she said.

"Don't worry, pet," said Victor. "We've still got Dudley, a little piece of Caroline. We could even look after Dudley while Albert finds work."

Louise looked up hopefully through her tears.

"Would you want us to look after Dudley for you, Albert?"

"Maybe. But I would have to think about it first. I don't mind the idea of being a solo dad, really."

"Oh."

Louise looked a little taken aback. Perhaps Victor had been a little too blunt about Albert finding work. She would so much love to take Dudley home to Staffordshire and spoil him to bits. And she could see that they would have to try and be a little bit more diplomatic about things in the future.

Upstairs, a couple of detectives were making a final survey of the main bedroom and the bathroom where Caroline had died. They had taken note of everything present…the folded newspapers, the poppy seeds, the bunches of garlic, the new mirror, the burned-out pink candle in the enamel candle-holder on the bathroom tiles, the small bottles of essential oils, the bathrobe, and what looked like guano on the floor. The bath was still filled with the original blood-tinged bathwater and the bathroom mirror was watermarked with bloodstained soap suds.

The detectives took their final samples of bathwater and guano and then got ready to approach the family downstairs. In the meantime, Caroline's body had been taken to the morgue in Belfast for an autopsy. The more senior detective entered the living room first.

"Er, excuse me, Mr. Pengally and Mr. and Mrs. Mallory. We've taken our final samples and searched for fingerprints. No fingerprints I'm afraid. So far, it looks like—according to the forensics team—that Caroline might have had some sort of gastric upset from something she had eaten. They're still investigating that of course. Then again, she may have been overcome by the fumes of all those oils in the bathwater. We're going to have the bottles of essential oils analyzed, but even now it smells pretty strong up there. Then there is the question of the mark on her neck. We think it may be an animal bite of some sort. We're having the guano analyzed and also checking to see how much blood she lost. The forensics say there might have been a certain amount of anemia—that still has to be confirmed—but the bruises point to evidence of a struggle. They're trying to work out whether the main cause of death was anemia or drowning. Or it could have been a combination of both."

"So, what sort of animal may have been involved?" asked Victor.

"We're not at liberty to say, sir, but off the record I heard someone in forensics discussing vampire bats."

"Vampire bats?" Victor repeated incredulously.

"Yes. Apparently, they're quite small but they can jump up at you like a catapult off the ground."

"But what about the bruising?"

"As I say, they're still working on it, but it definitely looks as though a struggle took place."

"That's incredible!" said Louise.

"Apparently, the chief inspector will be contacting one of the zoologists attached to the London Zoo for further information. That's as much as I can tell you at present."

"Oh well, thank you sir," said Albert, standing up to shake his hand. "Will you keep us informed of any further developments?"

"Of course, Mr. Pengally. Glad to be of service."

Albert showed the two detectives out and then re-entered the lounge deep in thought. *Vampire bats? Anemia?* he thought to himself. *This sounds pretty suspicious, especially with that mark I saw on Caroline's neck. There's something more to this, but I don't know what.*

As if reading his thoughts, Louise said, "Strange, you know. Victor had anemia a while back. You remember, it was back in September, wasn't it Victor, at the Abbots Bromley Horn Dance. It was all in the papers. But of course, you heard about it Albert. Victor got that card from Caroline just afterward."

"Yes, that's right. We heard all about that over here. We knew Victor was involved. Terrible, wasn't it? And the horns had to be sawn off from that jester guy's stomach. He was gored after tripping over some kid and Victor had an attack of anemia…that's right. But you look okay now," he said, eyeing Victor up and down.

"I'm fine now. It only lasted about a month right up to the day of the accident. Neville, the jester…he was Caroline's ex-boyfriend."

Albert looked stunned.

"Ex-boyfriend?" he repeated, stumbling over the words distastefully.

"Yes, Neville was going out with Caroline before she met you."

Albert did another double-take. "Strangely enough," Victor went on, "I would feel ill whenever Neville was around but now that he's gone, I'm right as rain, touch wood."

"Very odd," agreed Albert. "So, whereabouts was this Neville chap buried, or was he cremated?"

"He was buried in St Nicholas's churchyard in Abbots Bromley, wasn't he, Louise?"

"That's right. Huge funeral. Loads of people spilling out of the church and onto the street. Victor and his Morris dancers were pallbearers, weren't you love?"

"Yes. Neville's father more or less insisted that we were. Their whole family was devastated. And you can imagine how I felt! As guilty as hell. But it was all an accident. Just a sheer fluke. It could never happen again."

"Were this guy Neville and Caroline very close?" Albert asked Louise tentatively.

"They were engaged to be married at one stage," said Louise.

"Oh…so that's who he was. Her ex-fiancé. Now I follow you. It's all starting to make more sense now."

Victor and Louise looked at one another. There was a long pause. Albert's 'numbskull' mind was working overtime. Even his father-in-law would have been impressed if he knew what was going on in his mind. Albert decided to have a talk to his brother, Ed, after the funeral.

*

Two days later the forensic police had analyzed the results and released the body to a local funeral parlor in Belfast. A zoologist from London Zoo whose specialty was bats had positively identified the mark on Caroline's neck as the sign of a bite from a vampire bat. There had been no reports of vampire bats escaping from any local zoos, but the peculiar thing was that these creatures were normally found living in tropical and sub-tropical regions like Central and South America. The question was how could one have possibly found its way to Northern Ireland? Unless someone was keeping them as unlawful pets…

The zoologist reported that when people get attacked, the only evidence of the visit is usually the discovery of a small cut and blood-soaked sheets the next morning. If you're unlucky, paralytic rabies can develop three weeks later. Bats can return night after night, he said, if the victim is a convenient one, and bats have been known to actually move their roosts closer to their victims. He stated that due to a diet exclusively of blood (a sanguivory diet), these vampire bats have the fewest teeth of all bats. They have an anticoagulant in their saliva which prevents blood from congealing and there is also an anesthetic in their saliva which prevents the victim becoming irritated by the bite.

He also reported that vampire bats can drink up to twelve tablespoons (or one and a-half times their weight) of blood at one sitting. They fly in search of a victim and prey on sleeping animals and even people. They can jump up off the ground and use the heat sensors on their noses to help them locate a vein close to the skin. Then with their very sharp teeth they make a small cut in the victim's skin and squat down to lap up the blood as it trickles slowly down from the throat. Within twenty minutes, the bat would have finished its meal, he said. And finally, he mentioned that if a vampire bat doesn't find a feed for several nights in a row, it will die of starvation. Hence the evidence of the regurgitation practice from a parent to its young.

The guano droppings, needless to say had been analyzed as containing evidence of blood products and were very much the same in every other way as normal droppings from bats known to be vampire bats.

The forensic team also found evidence from Caroline's stomach contents of acute gastritis due to eating oysters the night before. And there was an irritation of her nostrils due to inhaling too strong a concentration of essential oils. There was also a marked state of acute anemia and traces of anticoagulant and anesthetic in her blood, indicating a sanguivory bite. The bruises on her arms and legs indicated a struggle in the bath with someone or something stronger than herself. But the primary cause of death was found to be drowning.

The outcome of all this was that Albert was now the prime suspect, not only because he was Caroline's husband (the first normally to be questioned in a homicide) but also because of his rather unusual appearance and style of dress. He was definitely a very Gothic-looking character and could quite easily have passed for a witch, (which of course, he was.) And witches sometimes keep strange pets…

So it was, that he was taken to the local police station immediately for questioning.

"Now, Mr. Pengally," the sergeant said, "you are the deceased's legal husband, I believe?"

"Yes sir."

"And you work as…?"

"Unemployed sir," Albert corrected him.

"Oh, so you were married with a wife and child and no income? A beneficiary?"

"I have an inheritance which I share with my brother."

"And your parents?"

"Dead. They died in the 'troubles' some years ago. My father was a tax consultant and my mother a university lecturer."

"Oh, I am sorry." The inspector looked embarrassed and then asked, "Now where were you as a point of interest, on the night of your wife's suspected homicide?"

"I was at an indoor rugby union football tournament in Cardiff, Wales with my brother, Ed and some friends."

"I see. We will need to back up evidence from these people of course. Can you supply us with names and addresses?"

"Yes."

"Very good. Now, I would also like your permission for us to search your flat. Just routine, you know."

"Of course. Any time you like."

"This afternoon?"

It was agreed that three police officers would return with Albert to the flat straight away. Victor and Louise were at home with Dudley and were a little taken by surprise at the intrusion.

"Just routine, Mr. and Mrs. Mallory. We won't get too much in your way."

With that, Albert made a cup of tea for his in-laws while the officers searched the flat. Albert knew that as soon as they came across all his books, his wand, athame, herbs and candles in his study, that he would be questioned again. He was not wrong. The policemen soon reappeared and spoke to him in a serious tone. "We would like to take you back to the station for further questioning, if you don't mind, Mr. Pengally."

Obediently Albert left with them in the car to the police station for the second time, leaving Victor and Louise even more worried.

"Mr. Pengally," the chief inspector began. "We believe we have evidence to support the fact that you are a witch. Do you admit to this?"

"Yes, I'm a Wiccan, a white witch."

"Do you keep pets?"

"We have a black cat, Moggie."

"What about bats?"

"Bats? No, we don't keep bats."

"Then how do you explain the evidence of vampire bats in your bathroom on the night of your wife's homicide?"

"I don't know, sir."

"They were vampire bats, Mr. Pengally."

"So, you were saying."

"You know that vampire bats suck blood, don't you, Mr. Pengally?"

"Yes."

"Well, that was what they were sucking that night—blood. At around the same time as your wife's murder. How would you explain that?"

"I don't know, sir. I was away at the time."

"So, you say. But I'm sorry to say, Mr. Pengally, that you are our greatest suspect at present. We have no fingerprints as you know, but I would strongly recommend that you co-operate with us and do not do an overseas flit to Europe or anywhere exotic just at the present. We need your co-operation. So, what I would like you to do right now is just go down that hallway there to your right for a police medical. Just routine, you know. They need to check for any bruises."

"Yes, sir."

Albert shuffled down the hallway to where a male police officer was waiting for him with a stethoscope around his neck.

"Come in, Mr. Pengally, I've been expecting you. Just if you wouldn't mind removing everything except your underwear, and I'll be with you in a moment."

Albert sighed and looked at him with a bored expression as the officer turned to finish some paperwork.

"Be with you in a jiffy," the officer said as Albert disrobed. Then without looking up he asked, "Are you ready?"

"Yes," replied Albert resignedly.

The doctor stood up and went over to examine him more closely.

"Well, you look pretty good to me. Just turn around slowly and raise your arms. That's it. Now let's have a look at your legs." There was a pause. "Amazing. No bruises. Just like magic!" he said, smiling widely at his own joke. "That will be all, Mr. Pengally. It's as simple as that. I'll just sign this form and send you back to the chief inspector with it as soon as you're dressed."

When Albert delivered the form, the chief inspector did a double-take on reading the report and reluctantly showed Albert the door.

"Thank you, Mr. Pengally," he said. "We will be grateful for your co-operation at all times."

Albert smiled triumphantly, shook his hand, and was dropped back at the flat by police car.

"I'm off the hook!" Albert said proudly as he met Victor and Louise at the door. "No bruises you see."

"Oh, but that's terrible that they thought you were guilty!" Louise said, appalled.

"The husband's always suspect," Victor put in.

"Yes, but…Albert? Albert wouldn't hurt a fly, would you Albert?" Louise said.

"Not unless it was sucking my blood," Albert replied grimly.

9

Caroline's funeral was finally held a week later in early February at a small chapel attached to the Belfast Crematorium five miles from the city center in Northern Ireland. It had been decided that Belfast would be a more convenient venue than the Inishowen Peninsula, as the body had been held over at the morgue in Belfast and the crematorium was nearby.

Back in Abbots Bromley, the Mallorys' letterbox was becoming filled with sympathy cards, including one from the Yelavich family. Victor and Louise and Dudley were at the funeral in Ireland, as well as Albert and his identical twin brother, Ed and Ed's girlfriend, Alison. Then there was Davinia, Caroline's best friend and her young son, Liam. All of Albert's twenty-strong coven were there, as well as several of Caroline's aunts, uncles and cousins.

It was a blustery day and gray clouds swept in off the lough from the northeast. Rain threatened and it was cold. Although the crematorium was encircled by immaculate frost-covered lawns, beautiful camellias in bloom and was sheltered by belts of conifer trees, the small fountain outside the chapel was being whisked askew by the squally wind, so that the little cherub statue creating it seemed to be capable of amazing feats. However, inside the chapel it was cozy and warm and more serene. It was quite civilized really. The neo-pagans sat dressed in white on one side of the chapel and on the other side sat the Mallory family, (including Albert as a concession to them.)

The service was taken by a Wiccan high priestess especially brought in from the city center of Belfast for the occasion. Caroline's coffin was draped in a white lace shroud, white snow drops, sprigs of holly and white lilies. The music of Enya played softly in the background and four candles sat upon the altar.

The high priestess cleared a ritual space and then cast a circle widdershins, opening her arms wide. She invoked the four elements of earth, air, water, and fire and then religiously lit the four candles as beacons to the north, south, east, and west. Prayers were recited to the gods and to the spirits of departed ancestors and then Davinia gave a moving eulogy, telling of her friendship with Caroline since they were six years old. Their lives had seemed to have moved in a kind of parallel fashion.

Finally, the coffin was slowly lowered down and away to the crematorium behind a pair of royal blue velvet curtains to the haunting tones of the Pan pipes. White wine and cakes baked with wheat were served to the gathering and then everyone withdrew to a large lounge for a private reception.

Louise leaned heavily on Victor and Albert for support throughout. Caroline's death seemed to have brought them closer together somehow. She was an only child, wife, and mother who, at only twenty, they had just farewelled forever. There were tears that flowed, but nothing that a little white wine wouldn't help fix. Once they had composed themselves a little more and they were out of earshot of Albert, Louise said to Victor while patting his arm:

"There you are now. That wasn't too painful, was it, for a Wiccan funeral I mean? Did you notice that the lady speaker mentioned the 'Horned One'? Just like in the history of the Abbots Bromley Horn Dance. So really, you have already been initiated into pagan culture yourself without realizing it. And Wicca is a form of paganism."

"You are a clever little deductionist today, aren't you?" said Victor, grinning. "Yes, I suppose I am a pagan at heart, but not a Wiccan. I don't believe in spells and things."

"But spells are just prayers."

"Maybe. But what about broomsticks?"

"None of them can fly…Albert says they just represent male and female parts. The brush is the female bit and the stick is the male bit. Just like how Morris dancers dance with sticks. It's a male thing."

Victor looked at her with his mouth agape.

"You are clever today, aren't you? I suppose it's because you're female."

They looked at each other and laughed.

"Let's have another drink," said Victor.

*

Meanwhile, Albert had been talking to Davinia beside a huge flower arrangement at the foot of a bronze statue of Pan and his pipes that he had hired especially for the occasion. He spotted his brother Edwin and his girlfriend Alison and waved them over. Edwin was of course an identical twin and so had the exact appearance of his brother, except that he had slightly shorter hair and appeared to be a little more 'switched on'. Alison was a brunette with long, straight hair and very direct blue eyes. Introducing the two girls, Albert then took Edwin aside.

"Ed, me old mate, I need to talk to you in private. I suppose it goes without saying that I'm suspect number one with the police in all this. Anyway, I've got them stumped at the moment because I've got no bruises, which the murderer has to have. Anyway, I think I know who did it."

He looked up to check that no one was listening in.

"You know how Victor got tied up in that Abbots Bromley Horn Dance accident back in September?"

"Yes."

"Well, the jester guy, the one that was killed, he was Caroline's ex-fiancé."

"Really!"

"Yes, and you know how Victor was very anemic before and at the accident? Well, he said it was the jester guy—Neville's his name—who was making him anemic. It was only ever when he was nearby. It was like his energy was being sapped apparently."

"So, what are you saying?"

"Well, Caroline died from drowning primarily, but she was also found to be extremely anemic. A vampire bat bite mark was found on her neck they said, and they found droppings on the floor."

"No!"

"Yes. So, what I'm saying is that that Neville guy is highly suspicious. In my opinion, that bite was not necessarily from a bat. Vampire bats were present in the bathroom at the time of Caroline's death because droppings were found as evidence. But in my opinion, speaking from the occult knowledge I have as a Wiccan, that bite was from a real vampire."

Edwin looked at his brother blankly.

"You reckon?"

"I reckon. How else could she have got all those bruises and a bite causing that much blood loss? I reckon bloody Neville came back from his grave to get her."

"Shit! Why?"

"She dumped him for me, remember?"

"So, what are you going to do?"

"You and me, my old son, are going to stake the guy."

Ed looked at Albert with consternation and stammered incoherently as he pointed erratically between the two of them. "You…and…m…me?"

"Yep."

"When?"

"Next Saturday night."

"But…"

"No buts, mate. We're doing it."

Ed looked a bit lost for words.

"Okay. Only because it's for you then. Where's the guy buried?"

"In the cemetery of St Nicholas's Church in Abbots Bromley."

"Oh, shit. That's miles away."

"Sorry, that's where he is."

"Okay, but I'll have to call in to Cardiff on the way. I left a T-shirt autographed by Brian O'Driscoll at Callum's flat. That won't be a problem, will it?"

"Aw…no."

"Okay, then. You're on."

"Right, then. I'll phone you tomorrow after the funeral."

The two young men then returned to where they had left Davinia and Alison talking together. Davinia was restraining her young Liam from eating a poppy from out of the cornucopia of flowers spilling around the feet of the statue.

"Don't eat *that*, Liam," she said. "You never know what's in it. All kinds of opium and stuff probably."

Alison laughed and said, "Whenever Albert and Caroline used to bring Dudley to visit, he was no problem at all. But I suppose once they reach Liam's age, that's when they're into everything."

"Exactly. I can't turn my back without something going on. Just wait till it's your turn."

"Oh, I can't see that happening for a while," said Alison. "Edwin's far too busy with his job at the tax department and I work from home as a commercial artist. We're not married or anything like that, just living together. Edwin's quite different from his twin brother really. He's got more of a work ethic whereas Albert's more laid back and more of a drifter. But he's really into the craft in a big way, is our Albert. He organized most of the funeral today."

"Yes," Davinia agreed. "It was a nice service, wasn't it? Different. Very 'au naturel'."

*

The next day, Albert phoned Edwin as promised, but from a call box, just to be on the safe side.

"Are you still game?"

"To be sure. One thing that's been bugging me though. Did Victor have any bite marks at all himself?"

"Not that I know of. But modern-day living vampires can drain your energy and make you anemic just by standing next to you. They don't have to physically bite unless they're in the undead form, according to my sources."

"I see. Alright. Lead on McDuff."

"Okay. Now a Saturday night is the only night that vampires are meant to stay in their graves. So, can you meet me on Saturday night in Staffordshire, Abbots Bromley at the Grosvenor Motel in Surrey Street at 8 pm? It's unit two. I'll bring a couple of pairs of gumboots and parkas and a stake and shovels in the van. And gloves. I'll take the Superseacat over to Heysham from Belfast and then drive down the rest of the way to Abbots Bromley and meet you there."

"Okay. What shall I bring?"

"Just yourself."

"Okay."

"One other thing…"

"Yes?"

"Wear your underpants inside out. It's traditional when you're vanquishing vampires."

"What…? Are you kidding?"

"No, mate, I'm not."

*

The day before D-Day arrived and Albert had decided to act as 'solo dad' and keep Dudley with him in Londonderry for the past few days. Victor and Louise had sadly gone home empty-handed without their little grandson. They knew he would be in good hands with Albert, but they were not to know that Albert had since parked Dudley with Ed's girlfriend, Alison in Letterkenny, while he and his twin brother traveled separately to Abbots Bromley in Staffordshire, England. Albert left on Friday morning on the Superseacat from Belfast to Heysham and Edwin left at the same time from Belfast airport for Cardiff in Wales. They would meet up at Abbots Bromley's Grosvenor Motel at 8 pm on Saturday night, Albert traveling in his van and Edwin by public transport.

At eight o'clock, Edwin arrived at the rendezvous and Albert let him inside.

"Well timed, mate. Good to see ya. Are you all psyched up?"

"As much as I'll ever be."

"Good. We'll go in my van at around eleven o'clock. I've got a torch and other bits and pieces if we need them. Did you collect your T-shirt?"

"Yes. Signed and sealed by the man himself. Could be worth a bit in years to come. Oh, and I caught the train from Cardiff up to Manchester and bused across from there. No problems."

"Good. Now I'll just show you this rough map I've made so we can see exactly where we're going from here…"

*

At eleven o'clock, the twins drove the van out to the cemetery at St Nicholas's Church. The moon was in its first quarter so there was just enough light for them to work without fear of discovery. They searched among the tombstones by torchlight until they came to one inscribed:

'Here lies Neville Yelavich

1974–2000

May he Rest in Peace'

"This is it!" said Albert. "Mind those rose bushes there at either end. We don't want to leave samples of blood on the prickles."

"Hey, look at all those little round holes around the grave in this slushy snow!" remarked Edwin.

"Aha! A sure sign that a vampire lives here!" said Albert.

"Is that right?" said Edwin. "I believe you."

"Let's just start digging, but very neatly. We don't want to make it look like the grave's been tampered with."

The twins began their gruesome task, silently digging in the cold dark night. An owl hooted nearby and flapped overhead. The ground was quite hard under a covering of melting snow and slush. Albert stopped for a rest.

"Lucky the moon isn't full. If any moonlight fell on him, the bugger would be resurrected. But we still have to be careful. I've brought a big sheet of polythene to keep any moonlight off him."

They kept on digging and by eleven thirty the coffin was unearthed. Neville would be waiting for them inside, asleep in his coffin. It was now 8 February (a week since St Brigit's Day back in Ireland and it was also a major sabbat day in the Wiccan calendar—a time for the celebration of spring)—but the two Pengally boys hoped to be celebrating something else tonight.

They opened up the coffin and sure enough, there was Neville Yelavich lying there in all his glory and stinking to high heaven. By torchlight, his skin was quite ruddy, his body bloated and his arms appeared to move slightly. This was all due of course to blood pooling in the capillaries, methane gas, and the expansion of gases in decomposition. Bright red blood oozed from his mouth and nose due to the cold temperature and his eyes opened and shut as if he were blinking.

"Shit! He bloody blinked at me!" exclaimed Edwin.

"Remember what I told you before, Ed. All is not what it seems. It's the gas in there."

"Oh, right."

Albert was not perturbed by any of this. He knew all these things to be natural occurrences.

"This has got to be him," said Albert between his teeth. "Not that I ever met him. Filthy sod. Molesting my wife and then sucking the life out of her. Just give me that stake will you Ed? Keep the moonlight off him with that polythene too—I don't want him coming around. Just let's get this over with. Oh, I nearly forgot…the poppy seeds and garlic first, that's right."

He gingerly sprinkled the seeds and garlic cloves all over the body and then took hold of the wooden stake in between his two gloved hands. He stood over the coffin and raised the stake high about his head. Then with an almighty thrust, he drove it hard into Neville's heart.

"God, send you burst!" he incanted. "Bastard!" he muttered.

Blood spurted out at once all over the place and spattered Albert's parka.

"Just to make doubly sure, I'll do it again."

This time he staked Neville's throat. A preternatural groan emanated from Neville's vocal cords as the gas was pressured through his glottis.

"Filthy swine! Now where's that spade again? Oh yes!"

He removed the stake from Neville's throat and laid it beside the body. Then he took an almighty swipe with the spade and Neville was decapitated.

"It would be good if we could burn him too, to really finish him off, wouldn't it?" said Edwin.

"Yes, but we don't want to get caught lighting fires, do we? This is a crime, remember, interfering with the dead in their graves."

"Okay, okay, I know. Did I get any blood on me?"

"Just on your parka, same as me I think."

"Good. I don't want to go down under one of those vampire curses. But I've still got my undies on inside out, so I should be all right. You?"

"Of course, I have. I wouldn't let you down."

"Good. Right then. Let's stuff his mouth with garlic and rebury the bugger."

"Okay mate."

They scurried around preparing the body for reburial before anyone could find them getting up to mischief. They were both wearing black so that was good camouflage on a relatively moonless night. In another half an hour, they were done. The coffin had been reburied as neatly as possible, and the clods of earth had been put back together as tidily as a completed jigsaw puzzle. No one would ever notice that the grave had been consecrated unless they were extremely particular.

They traipsed back through the slushy graveyard to the van, reloaded the shovels and made it back to the motel. Soon they were enjoying hot showers and hot cocoa and congratulating themselves on a job well done. They raised their mugs in the air, toasted each other and patted themselves on the back.

"He won't be out on the prowl anymore," Albert said.

"That's one less vampire prowling the face of the earth!" agreed Edwin.

The next morning, they were up at 5 am so that Albert could catch the eight o'clock high-speed sea service ferry from Holyhead to Dun Laoghaire in Dublin. Albert would drop Edwin off in Liverpool on the way so that they would arrive home in Ireland separately. This would also give Edwin more time to visit another friend in England.

10

By around ten o'clock the next morning, Albert was in Dun Laoghaire, Dublin. Edwin had been safely dropped off in Liverpool and was finding his way around before visiting friends and then catching a flight back from there to Belfast. Albert with his vanload of incriminating evidence wrapped in black polythene had decided to steer clear of the Northern Ireland route and take the safe road back through Sligo. You could never be too careful if you were riddled with guilt, and he wasn't going to take any chances. The inside of his van looked just like any other handyman's van, with toolkit, ladders, boots, fishing rod etcetera and it had not aroused any suspicion when he had landed in Dun Laoghaire, much to his relief.

He took the M4 highway out of Dublin and then got onto the N4 toward County Westmeath. He was relieved that he had avenged Caroline's death and glad that he had dispatched her murderer as he lay in his coffin. He lit a cigarette to try and settle his nerves and to calm his mind as he traveled further out into the countryside. He turned on the radio and listened moodily to some lachrymose Country and Irish music echoing tinnily over the airwaves while his fingers played absentmindedly on the steering wheel. It was squally with bursts of rain outside, so he was constantly monitoring the windscreen wipers to clear his view and to help clear his mind. All he had to do now was dump the evidence somewhere and then get back to Ed's place as soon as possible, clean up the van so that it was spick and span, and collect Dudley. He whistled optimistically to the music and stepped a little harder on the accelerator.

Suddenly he did a double-take. A signpost on his right was pointing northward to the town of Trim. He suppressed a grin as the memory came flooding back. It was several summers ago now that he and an old girlfriend had visited Trim Castle near where they hold a bizarre summer horserace with nuns as jockeys. It's called the 'Nuns' Run'. His ex—Julie was her name— had bribed one of the nuns into swapping her clothes for a habit. To this day, he still didn't know how she managed it. But it certainly wasn't just for a taste of her candy floss. She ended up winning the race. He smirked at the memory and wondered what Julie was up to now…

Just then, a loud roar in his right ear almost knocked him out of the driver's seat. A huge lorry drew up beside him, accelerated, changed gears with an ear-splitting graunch and then passed. Albert ignored the effrontery. He must have slowed down without realizing it while he was daydreaming. It was not long before he was at Kinnegad where the road forked. One of the side roads here, he remembered, a few miles outside Kinnegad, featured a sacred tree. Itinerants (the so-called 'tinkers') still tied ribbons to it as they passed. It was supposed to bring them luck. *Perhaps that's what I should do now,* thought Albert…*just duck down that side road and tie a ribbon to that tree. I might be needing a little luck of my own in all this!*

He had seen one or two of the tinkers' horse-drawn carriages around, but they were fast becoming a thing of the past. These days they were more likely to be speeding along in old cars drawing a caravan with a TV aerial sticking out of the roof. Their stock in trade though still tended to be the 'colored' or piebald ponies which they grazed along the roadside and sold around the country. The tinkers traveled from one end of the country to the other and tended to meet up at places like Killoglen's Puck Fair where a wild Billy goat is crowned king for three days, or other such fairs. Albert still found it hard to believe that the ancestors of these tireless travelers were not related to Romany gypsies, but descended from an ancient indigenous people who preferred a wandering life to a sedentary life in the villages.

Checking his map, Albert took the righthand fork through central Westmeath, stepped on the accelerator and passed the previously offending lorry. Satisfied with that little maneuver, he then settled back in his seat and turned up the music some more. It was not long before he was passing Lough Owel in this land of bogs, lakes, streams, and old canals. He could even smell the turf smoke filtering into his van as he passed some of the houses dotted about the place.

Just prior to reaching the little town of Ballinalack, he hung a right turn down a side road leading off to Lough Derravaragh. He had a delivery to make. The road was a bit bumpy in places the closer he got to his destination. He found a private spot near where the River Inny joined the lough, checked that the coast was clear, and then hoisted his fishing rod and polythene package of digging gear over his shoulder. If anyone were to ask him what he was doing, he would say he was going fishing. Finding a likely spot with relatively deep water and checking once again that no one was around, he let slip the black package into the water. That little task now completed, he picked up his fishing rod and headed back to the van. Now all he wanted to do was make a quick getaway. He revved up his motor and was soon back on track heading toward Sligo.

Along the way he couldn't help thinking about the long cool Guinness he would have when he finally arrived home. He deserved it he felt, after such a stressful weekend. He would desist from stopping at a pub along the way as he hadn't yet finished the job at hand. It was fortunate that drinking was allowed on Sundays in the Republic and yet he hadn't even taken up the opportunity. The pubs would be closed back home in Northern Ireland. Not that he was one to drink and drive.

His mind wandered wistfully back to the trips they used to make as young children to Galway to visit his maternal grandparents. His grandfather was a practiced distiller of poteen, a colorless moonshine made from potatoes. But his motive was more tipsifactory than epicurean and it tasted more of bog-heather to Albert. In spite of this, his grandfather always used to proclaim with a mischievous smile on his face and in his high-pitched tenor voice that it 'tasted like a little bit of Heaven and a little bit of Hell'.

About an hour later, Albert reached Sligo, the dream holiday destination of his teenage years. The verdant countryside and the capricious looking sky blowing in from the Atlantic was a sight to behold. The flat-topped Ben Bulben Mountain stood sentinel as always to the north and Knocknarea mountain to the west. He and Edwin had played many a round of golf upon the sprawling seaside links at Rosses Point and had climbed Knocknarea often to view the mythical Queen Maeve of Connaught's tomb. She was supposed to lie under forty thousand tons of stones that formed a cairn atop the broad, flat surface of the mountain. Local legend had it that if you brought a stone to the top of the mound, your troubles would be lessened. However, it was important not to subtract any stones from the mound for fear of Queen Maeve's wrath! The legend of her death is quite bizarre. She is said to have been killed by a slingshot consisting of a piece of hard cheese that was fired by her nephew. If you walk right around the top of the mountain, you can look down on Standhill

Airport and watch planes landing and taking off—a sight sure to keep teenage boys occupied for hours.

Once he was out of Sligo, Albert carried on in a north easterly direction until he reached Ballyshannon, where he stopped for refreshments at a petrol station. There was no international folk festival to be had here on this wet, wintry day (not that he would have had time to attend anyway) so Albert was soon on his way again through the towns of Donegal and Ballybofey before coming upon the familiar sight of the ever-present Gothic tower of St Eunan's Cathedral in Letterkenny.

Albert was never so glad to see his brother's girlfriend in Letterkenny as then. He was especially glad to be reunited with little Dudley. However, first he must clean out the van and then he could travel back home to Londonderry with Dudley and partake of that nice cool Guinness. No matter how hard he tried to hide it, that gory staking had taken its toll on him. But was it worth it?

"You bet!" he said to himself. "No wife of mine is going to be interfered with and killed by a bloody vampire!"

11

That same Sunday afternoon, the police in Abbots Bromley got a tipoff. It was one of the Yelavich sisters, Griselda, the elder one. Neville's grave had been tampered with, she said. There were signs of a disturbance upon her last visit there that afternoon. She had found that the top slab of the grave was slightly askew and there was evidence that the ground may have been dug up around the headstone.

Upon inspection by other family members and the police, it was decided that at least two able-bodied men would have been required to shift the top slab. Mr. Yelavich was horrified and asked that the grave be dug up and inspected immediately. It was atrocious to think that someone should interfere with his son's grave.

"Whoever committed this unforgivable sin should have to pay for it," he proclaimed.

Consequently, gravediggers were organized to raise the coffin on Monday morning to inspect its contents in case of sabotage. A crowd of interested onlookers had gathered in the churchyard on the day the coffin was to be unearthed because nothing like this had ever happened in Abbots Bromley before. The young guy who was in the local pub with the girl with the orange spiky hairdo was in among the small gathering. "How much do you bet?" he asked her again.

"Fifty pounds that he wasn't a vampire like you said he was."

"Okay. Shake."

They shook hands and waited in eager anticipation. All was to be revealed in an hour. The coffin was raised and opened. The evidence spoke for itself. Neville's body lay staked and decapitated in all its glory. Once the news got past the police barrier, there was a collective 'Ooh!' from the crowd. The police had to restrain the small but feisty group of onlookers who were straining their necks to get a look.

"Back, thank you, back. This isn't a ghoul show!" they barked.

"Mr. Yelavich? I'm sorry. What can I say…?" said the head policeman.

"I am stung. Stung beyond belief. Who would stoop so low as this? Such an archaic practice reeks of evil!" Mr. Yelavich was absolutely livid with anger and was shaking uncontrollably. He needed to be supported by his two daughters. "We—and I am speaking for the whole Yelavich family here—we want our retribution," he thundered.

Unperturbed by this outburst, several newspaper men hovered around the edge of the crowd like vultures while the police sifted through the remains of the evidence. The grave itself was left with two guards and the stake was taken away for analysis. As the crowd slowly dispersed, savoring this hot piece of news, the guy from the pub was heard to say to his lady friend with the spiky hairdo, "You owe me fifty pounds, thank you."

"Oh, tush! You can take me out to dinner on it then!"

The journalists made a meal of it, too, with headlines in the evening papers reading:

'GRAVE DESECRATED BY VAMPIRE HUNTERS' and 'JESTER GAROTTED IN OWN GRAVE'.

It was the talk of the town in Abbots Bromley and rumors were rife that Neville had, in fact been a vampire and that was why Victor Mallory had been so anemic last September. This was all quashed by the realists who said it was all speculation and circumstantial evidence. There was much argument in the village between the two factions—vampirists and non-vampirists, and even pagans and non-pagans, Christians and non-Christians. Even black and white couldn't help but become involved. Everyone had something to say about it, no matter who they were. In the meantime, Neville's exhumed remains had been taken to the morgue in Manchester for further forensic examination. Somebody had hung a pair of antlers over his headstone in the cemetery as well. Perhaps it was someone from the Morris dancing group who had put them there in remembrance of his contribution to the Abbots Bromley Horn Dance. It was a fitting tribute.

*

News like this travels quickly, so it was not long before Albert was being contacted by the police in Northern Ireland again. He had hardly been back a day when he was recalled. The connection had since been made by the police between Albert, Victor, Neville, and Caroline. They found there was a link between the accidental killing of Neville Yelavich at the Abbots Bromley Horn Dance in September by Victor Mallory, and a link between the suspicious homicide of Victor Mallory's daughter, Caroline, possibly with Victor's son-in-law, Albert, who was a Wiccan. But just what was the connection? They meant to find out.

"Mr. Pengally, Neville Yelavich was the ex-fiancé of your late wife, we understand?"

"Yes, that is correct, sir."

"Was there ever any animosity between you and Neville Yelavich?"

"No, sir. I never even met the guy."

"Where were you on the evening of Saturday 8th February, Mr. Pengally?"

"I was at my brother Ed's in Letterkenny," he lied.

"Oh? And what were you up to there may I ask?"

"I was visiting my little son, Dudley, who was being looked after by Ed's girlfriend, Alison there."

"And why was your son being looked after there in Letterkenny?"

"To give me a break. I'm a solo dad."

"Of course. I'm sorry. Your wife was recently murdered, wasn't she? Only last week, it was." He cleared his throat. "That must have been a shock for you." There was a pause. "Mr. Pengally, we have reports that a person matching your description was seen entering the Grosvenor Motel at Abbots Bromley on that Saturday night at 8 pm."

"Oh, that would have been my twin brother, Ed. We're identical twins. He went over that way to visit friends in Cardiff, Staffordshire, and Liverpool, so I believe. He's a footie fanatic. We both are. He went over to collect a souvenir he left behind at the last match we went to in Wales in January."

"There was no special match this last weekend was there?"

"Er, no, sir."

"And what might your brother's address be in Letterkenny?"

"29 Kenty Avenue, sir."

"Thank you, Mr. Pengally. That will be all for now. We will be in touch."

Albert breathed a sigh of relief and showed the policeman out his front door. He had to contact his brother Ed fast, but he would not phone from home in case his phone was tapped. He found a phone booth and called his brother's cell phone number. He was in a pub in Liverpool and there was quite a bit of background noise.

"Ed! Albert here. I've just had the fuzz around. They're checking our alibis for Saturday night. They've discovered that the grave's been tampered with and they exhumed the body this morning. You've seen the papers? Yes, well I've told them I was at your place in Letterkenny checking on Dudley with Alison and that it was you only that they saw at the Grosvenor at eight o'clock on Saturday night. I said you were over that way visiting friends for a long weekend. And I told them about the T-shirt as well, okay?"

"Okay."

"Anything else that crops up, just let me know."

"Right. Better go. It's a bit noisy in here. Don't worry. I'll be back home with Alison late tonight. See you later."

Albert wrapped his coat around him and dashed home to his flat.

God, that was close, he thought. *At least, we used rubber gloves and wore gumboots. As long as no one saw us together, we should be okay.*

*

Back in Abbots Bromley, the Mallorys also found themselves being interviewed by the police. There was a knock at the front door and Louise answered it.

"Er, Abbots Bromley police. Mr. and Mrs. Mallory, I believe?"

"Yes."

"Just in connection with the exhumation this morning in St Nicholas's Church graveyard. May we come in? Mr. Mallory is here?"

"Yes, come in. Mr. Mallory is here."

Louise showed the two policemen into the lounge, where Victor was watching TV.

"Mr. Mallory. Just a few routine questions if you don't mind."

"Certainly. Take a seat."

"Mr. Mallory, is it true that you were suffering from anemia on the day of Neville Yelavich's death on the day of the Horn Dance last September?"

"Yes, sir."

"I believe, Mr. Mallory, that your daughter Caroline herself actually died in a homicide of drowning and secondary anemia only about two weeks ago in Ireland. Is that correct?"

"Yes, sir."

"A most unfortunate incident. Can you tell me if there is a family history of anemia?"

"Not as far as I know sir. No one else in the family has ever had it."

"We believe there may be some connection between the incident of Neville Yelavich's death and this recent desecration of his grave. Would you have any objection if we searched your flat?"

"Not at all, sir."

Finding nothing of any consequence except a couple of blonde, curly wigs which elicited the question from the younger policeman, "Do you happen to suffer from alopecia at times, Mrs. Mallory?"

Louise shook her head.

The two policemen soon left, none the wiser, or so Victor hoped. Ignoring the policeman's parting quip, Louise asked, "What can they hope to find here of any consequence? We've done nothing wrong. I wonder if Albert should know about this. I'd better ring him."

"If he's involved in any of this, he's stupider than I thought," said Victor.

"Hush, dear."

Louise got on the phone to Albert in Londonderry to tell him of the desecration of Neville's grave and to warn him that because of the family connection he may get a visit from the police just as they had themselves.

"Oh, they've already been!" said Albert. "In fact, they've been around twice today. They checked out the flat, the garage, the van, you name it. They just left a few minutes ago laden down with a whole lot of stuff from out of my study—sword, staff, athame, wand, pentacle, stone, and chalice. I mean to say, what are they going to do with all of that? It's no use to anyone at all except me!"

"I hope you're not involved in any of this stuff at the graveyard, Albert," said Louise.

"Not directly," said Albert evasively, as he was not to know whether his phone was being tapped.

"Why don't you come over and visit us and bring Dudley? I know you and Victor don't get on all that well, but he's at work most of the time and it would be a nice change for you."

"Oh no, Mrs. Mallory. I couldn't really." He didn't like to mention that he had only just returned from that very place in Staffordshire just a day ago and that his brother was still on the way back. "I can always go up to my brother's place if I need a break."

"It must be very quiet and lonely for you now, I'm sure. You know you're always welcome here anytime."

"Thank you, Mrs. Mallory. I must go now, Dudley's up to mischief."

Albert put down the phone.

"Jeez, those police move fast!" he said under his breath. "I'd better warn Ed and Allison of a possible search in Letterkenny as well. Not that they'll find anything there."

*

Over at the morgue in Manchester, Neville's remains were being combed for clues. The garlic stuffed in his mouth had been checked for fingerprints but there were none. The stake beside the body likewise showed a lack of fingerprints. The police had footprints of size 12 gumboots at the scene of the crime however. Only one set of footprints had been found, indicating that only one person was involved, but two people would have been required to shift the top slab of concrete off the grave. They deduced that in that case, the two people must have had the same sized feet—twins, perhaps?

Albert and Edwin thus became highly suspect by the police, especially as Albert was a Wiccan and because of his possible connection with his wife's murder and his father-in-law's accidental killing of Neville as well. But when the police checked the twins' shoe sizes, they were found to be a mere size ten. (Albert had deliberately bought two new pairs of gumboots from Selfridges two sizes too big so they could wear plenty of pairs of socks inside them to keep warm.)

Albert had already disposed of the two shovels, rubber gloves, and the two pairs of gumboots from the boot of his van in a quiet bog beside River Issy in Westmeath on the way back to Londonderry from Belfast. They were wrapped in black polythene, together with their two bloodied parkas, and he had watched as they sank like stones. Albert was meticulous in checking there were no bloodstains inside the van and had cleaned it inside and out at Ed's place before taking it back home to Londonderry. At any rate, he was not back home until at least five o'clock on the Sunday afternoon.

The twins' alibis could not be disproven by the police. Edwin's friend, Callum, in Cardiff confirmed that he had indeed collected the autographed T-shirt and then watched footie on TV before departing early to see other friends in Staffordshire and Liverpool. And Albert had told the police he had been visiting his son at Edwin's flat in Letterkenny. Alison had vouched for him there, so she was now in fact an accessory to the crime.

*

Meanwhile, back in Abbots Bromley, the Yelavich family were holding a special after-dinner memorial celebration of sorts in what they called their 'Red Room'. It was the exact antithesis and visual opposite of what thespians call their 'Green Room'. Mr. Yelavich had managed to procure for the family Neville's last painting from his night school class. It was an abstract nude on canvas painted in oils, cubism fashion. 'Nudism a la cubism', an experimental form that Neville was tinkering with before his untimely death. The painting was dominated by bright, garish colors and had been titled by him 'Carrie' and signed N. Yelavich 2000. Because it was his last and what Mr. Yelavich senior considered to be Neville's best painting, it was decided to hang it in the lounge as a tribute to him and to his ex-fiancée, Caroline Mallory—two young people whose lives had been taken tragically from them, prematurely.

He proposed a toast to his son, and the family all raised their glasses.

"To Neville, may he rest in peace," he said.

His wife and two daughters, Griselda and Esmée, repeated the toast and they all drank in silent homage to their lost son and brother.

12

Louise was posing in front of her bedroom mirror. She hadn't oiled herself up yet, but she had only one month to go before the next women's body building contest in Birmingham coming up in March. She took a deep breath and grimaced. "Grrr!" she said to herself in the mirror. "Now, I'll just try this one," she said, and turned side-on, drawing in her stomach so that her ribcage stuck out. Her little boobs lay flattened against her chest in her black bikini top and her tiny thong displayed plenty of muscular thigh and buttock down below. She put her arms behind her head and then raised them a little, cracking her knuckles together with a feigned smile. *Yes, I must remember to smile, mustn't I? Got to keep in with the punters,* she thought. Victor was in the lounge watching TV, so she thought she would ask his opinion on something.

"Victor, what do you think of this for a pose?"

She promptly fell into position like a lissome little puppet and held the pose until she got a reaction.

"Mmm…very nice, dear. What else have you got?"

She changed gear and flung herself into another avant-garde position so that all the muscles undulated right down her back, rippling as she flexed and unflexed.

"Mmm, I like it. Like the bikini too. Very itsy-bitsy. You don't think it's a bit small for public display?" he said, sounding slightly worried.

"No dear. All the other girls will be wearing their bikinis just as small. I have to keep up with the competition. Do you think I'll do okay?"

"I can't see why not. You did all right last time, and you seem to be sticking to that strict diet and the workout sessions, don't you?"

"Yes." She stood at ease and looked at him directly with one hand on her hip. "I'm just a bit apprehensive though. You know, with all that we've been through lately—Neville dying, you being in hospital, the fire and break-in by who-knows-what, shifting house, and Caroline being attacked and drowned in the bath for God's sake…not being allowed to babysit our own grandson, having our home searched and all this happening in the last six months! I think the cracks are starting to show in my performance a bit."

"Nonsense dear. Just keep focused. Treat it as relaxation. You do enjoy it, don't you?"

"Yes."

"Well, there you are then. Just keep practicing to your favorite music and you'll be fine."

"Mmm…the music does help. Same as with your Morris dancing, I suppose. Helps to keep your spirits up."

"That's more like it. Spoken like a real trouper."

They smiled and then Victor said, "Did you say you were making a cup of tea, love?"

"No, you big smoothie. But I will anyway because I've worked up a thirst myself now, believe it or not!"

"Good on you. I knew I could twist your arm."

Presently Louise returned with two piping hot cups of tea.

"Jesus, that's hot!" exclaimed Victor.

"It's because I'm so quick at making it," she explained. "You should wait for it to cool down a bit. Now what was I going to say? Oh yes. About Albert. I do wish he would come and stay and bring Dudley with him. He must be so lonely over there all on his own with just a baby for company. Don't tell me— I know you don't get on, but this really has got to stop. I mean, we don't want to lose our grandson, do we?"

"No, but that's beside the point. You see, I reckon that young Albert there has got tied up with this exhumation thing down at the cemetery. Now if he is involved, he won't want to be seen around here, will he? It stands to reason," he said.

"Yes, but he wouldn't do a thing like that would he? Dig up Neville's grave and interfere with the body?"

"He might. He *is* a witch, remember. And they can do some pretty weird stuff…"

"Mmm, but he's a good witch, love. Caroline was very happy with him, and he seems to be very good with Dudley from what I can tell."

"Yes, but remember if he did put a stake through Neville's heart—even though Neville was dead at the time—he would be up for mutilating a dead body. It would have been a husband's revenge against who he thought murdered his wife. But they haven't proved that Caroline was, in fact murdered yet. They say it was just a bat's bite and accidental drowning."

"Yes, a bat out of hell!" Louise said.

"No, you know what I mean Louise. If we speak rationally about the whole thing, Albert hasn't got a leg to stand on if he did it. So obviously, if he's responsible, he has to lie low. It makes sense to me."

"Yes, maybe you're right. We can't hope to expect too much. But Caroline and Albert didn't keep bats—any sort of bats—just a black cat, that's all." She paused reflectively. "But I would love to hold my little grandson once more. It's so hard now that we've lost Caroline, our only child…"

She began to weep into her tea. The strain was finally catching up with her. She had been stoical up till now but now she had to let it all out. It was a case of post-traumatic stress syndrome. Victor moved closer to her and put his arm around her.

"Yes, she was our little girl wasn't she love?" he said, silently wiping away a tear.

"But why should they pick on Albert?" Louise sobbed.

"Because Albert's a Wiccan and the police think that Albert thinks that Neville was a vampire. That's the crux of the matter."

*

Four weeks later, it was the night of Louise's competition in Birmingham. Quite a crowd had gathered in the auditorium and there was boisterous excitement in the air echoing through the stadium. Who was going to be overall men's champion tonight was what was on everyone's lips. Digger Dan or Phileous Romanoff? Both were real he-men with perfect physiques. Digger Dan was the smaller of the two men but possessed the bigger personality. He really played to the crowds and milked them for applause.

Then there was the women's section. There were six front runners and Louise was among them. She was wearing her silver lamé bikini tonight and the lucky charm that Victor had given her (a tiny ballet slipper on a chain around her neck.) She was busy psyching herself up out the back and practicing her breathing for the various poses that had been specially choreographed for her. She had got third place last time and she knew she could at least match that. She flexed and unflexed in front of the dressing room mirror and then her assistant, Sandy, entered to oil her skin with coconut oil. "Hi there, Sandy. Come in," Louise said.

"Ready for some oil? You've got some tough competition tonight, girl!"

"Oh, yes. I saw that Millie Brown was back again tonight, and Wendy Dennison."

"Yep, so we've got to make you look good so you can do your stuff and show them up. Turn around honey and I'll do your back first."

Louise did as she was told and leaned up against the doorway. Through her mind were going thoughts as if she were listening to a tape recorder... *'One, two, three, hold, flex, pump, pump, pump, relax, two, three, four, turn, and spring!'* She had a very good choreographer/trainer in Sharlene who was at that moment waiting outside in the wings to wish her luck before dashing back into the obscurity of the audience. Louise was reasonably confident that she could carry off all that she had been taught in the past few months. She had stuck religiously to the special carbohydrate diet of pasta and cereal and no sweets or alcohol for months, so she felt she deserved to do well.

"Turn around, hun, and I'll do your front."

Louise turned around and caught sight of her reflection in the mirror as she did so. *"Hmmm, not bad for a forty-year-old bird who's going places. You've got plenty of muscles, girl, just use them!"* she told herself silently.

Suddenly, the door opened. It was Sharlene, her choreographer.

"Good luck, Louise. They're just about to go on—the men, that is. I'll keep you posted. You're looking good, girl!"

"Thanks."

Louise heard muffled cheers inside her dressing room as the full complement of twelve men paraded across the stage. She could even hear some high-spirited, high-pitched women's voices yelling out, "Get your gear off!" and a bit of wolf whistling as well. She was nervous and excited at the same time and began her deep breathing exercises for the umpteenth time. Soon, she knew, she would be running the same gauntlet on stage, lined up 'meat-market fashion' with five other women in their string bikinis. She remembered the last time how the men went wild when she flaunted the tattoo on her left buttock at the audience. It was only a tattoo of a butterfly, but what the heck! She was just glad that Victor would be in the audience for moral support.

"You're done love," Sandy said, slapping Louise's buttock for luck.

"Oh thanks. Just listen to them out there will you! The audience is going crazy!"

"Sounds like they're all having a good time. Have you done your weigh-in yet? You don't look like you've put on an ounce of weight since the last competition."

"Yes, the weigh-in's all done. And I'm right on the limit of 110lbs, so everything's hunky dory."

"Great. Well, I'll wish you luck and get out of your way. Just yell if you need anything."

"Thanks, Sandy."

Sandy left to finish off oiling up the other contestants and Louise re-inspected her physique in the dressing room mirror. She was feeling full of energy because she had filled up her body with pasta during her pre-contest meal half an hour ago. Following that, she was not allowed even a glass of water in case it upset the weigh-in. Physically she looked strong, but was she up to it mentally? There was only one way to find out.

One hour later, Sharlene was back to report that Digger Dan had won the men's section again—that was two years in a row. It was his rakish humor that had helped him pip Phileous Romanoff to the post. Louise could hear the cheering from her dressing room.

"Okay, Louise. You're on. You all set?" called Sharlene's voice through the doorway.

"Yep."

"Okay, let's get you out there!"

Louise trooped onto the stage with the other women body builders and they all did a quick group display together for the crowd. There were more catcalls and wolf whistles. Then it was time for the individual items. Louise was the fourth to do her thing and waited her turn in the wings. When her signature tune played over the intercom to announce her item, she came alive as if a switch had been turned on. She had incorporated (with Sharlene's help) a little bit of aerobics as well as jazz-ballet into her routine. She showed off her nice calf and thigh muscles with a pose which involved doing the splits with her torso twisted and then flexing her pectorals and rotating her arms around her torso with tight fists. The lighting was synchronized with the music, which had a definite funky beat to it, and the steps she did were almost feline. She sprang into position and then pumped all her muscles in and out at the audience in time to the pulsing of the red strobe lights. She flashed her smile at the audience as she held each separate pose, and willed them with all her might to pick her. She drew sustenance from each wave of applause and carried on with renewed vigor to complete what she thought was one of her best performances. She was enjoying herself so much that before she knew it, her time was up. She bowed, waved and walked off.

"How did I do? How did I do?" she asked Sharlene backstage.

"Great! Just great!"

"Good!"

"Keep your fingers crossed, though, because Millie Brown and Wendy Dennison have yet to go on."

"Oh."

Louise went to her dressing room and wrapped herself in a white terry toweling bathrobe. She sat down in front of the mirror, dripping with perspiration and tried to relax. Her reflection stared back at her under the glare of the make-up lights.

"You look exhausted," she said to herself in the mirror.

She was dying for a cigarette, even though she hardly ever smoked. It was just the suspense getting to her. She found an old packet of Pall Mall in her bathrobe pocket and lit up. Nervously, she waited for the last two signature tunes to finish before the results could be announced. Then there was the sound of running footsteps down the corridor and a quick rap on the door. It opened and there was Sharlene.

"You're on again, love. They want you all on together while they choose a winner. Best of luck!"

"Thanks, Sharlene."

Louise quickly stubbed out her hardly touched cigarette and found herself lined up on stage again in the group display with the five other women. There were cheers and clapping and then when the microphone came on again, a hush fell over the audience and the judge stood up.

"Ladies and gentlemen. The winners for the Ladies' Section tonight of the Birmingham Body Builders Association are…Millie Brown, first, Wendy Dennison, second, and Francis Belton, third."

There was immediate wild applause, whistling and foot-stomping from the audience in response. The three winners were presented with their trophies and bouquets while the remaining contestants walked off in single file.

"Oh damn!" Louise said to herself. "That third prize was within my reach! Why didn't I get it? I could have beaten Francis Belton easily. I saw her perform last year and I didn't think she was that good. She must have improved since then because I know I haven't got worse! Damn, damn, damn!"

Sharlene came up to her backstage.

"Never mind Louise," she said. "You did your best I know. Better luck next time."

"Yes, thanks. I suppose Francis must have been just too good for me on the night."

"Mmm…Well, hang in there, kid."

Louise went back to her dressing room disappointed. She was hoping Victor would meet her there. If only she had been that little bit better…assuredly, Victor was waiting at the dressing room door and gave her a big hug.

"Fabulous! Fabulous, you were, darling!"

"Yes, but not fabulous enough!"

"Well, you have been under a great deal of pressure over the past six months. We both have. Something had to give and I guess this was it. But you did enjoy it, didn't you love?"

"Yes."

"Well then. That's all that matters, isn't it?"

They went in and each drew up a chair under the make-up lights. Victor poured them both a small brandy from a hip flask that he kept hidden in his coat pocket.

"You're pretty damn good for a feisty old grandmother of forty years old, you know!" he said, giving her a hug.

They had hardly had time to sit down when there was a knock on the dressing room door.

"Who is it?" Louise called.

"Some people to see you," Sandy replied. "They say they're from Morris dancing. Are you decent?"

"Yes."

"Okay."

The door opened and who should appear but Elspeth and Larry, beaming from ear to ear and holding a bottle of champagne between them.

"Hello, you two. What are you doing here?" Louise asked in surprise.

"We're just another couple of supporters," Elspeth said. "You were fantastic!"

"Yes, absolutely fantastic!" said Larry. "Victor told me you were performing tonight, so I thought Elspeth might like to come and see how it's done. You know, for when she retires…"

He ducked, playfully avoiding an imagined mugshot from either of the two women.

"Cheeky!" Elspeth said. "Pour us a drink, Dobbin, before I clobber you!"

13

St Patrick's Day, 17th March, the day sacred to the Irish, arrived and there was to be a rugby union football test match in Dublin with England versus the home side. The Pengally twins had decided they were not going to miss out on this major event come rain, hail or high water. It was a gray blustery spring day with light squally showers, typical of the weather that helps to keep the Irish countryside so green. But there were more bursts of green than usual today because not only was spring bursting out, but there were street parades everywhere. Screeds of people in the parades were wearing green. Even their pet dogs and hamsters wore green ribbons in their hair and little green jackets. Ice creams were green, lipstick was green, nail polish was green, hair was green and if you were lucky, your eyes were green or else you disguised the fact that they weren't with green contact lenses.

Albert picked up his brother from Letterkenny in his van and they drove the three hours to Dublin through the rain before booking into a motel. There was to be a party after the match at one of Albert's mates' places downtown. The twins anticipated it would be a riot because the home side was expected to win. They fortified themselves with a quick Guinness before walking the six blocks to the venue at Lansdowne Road, dressed in their supporting colors. As identical twins, they had dressed the same in white shirts, dark trousers, braces, dark green sports jackets, and green bow ties. And to top that off, they had each painted their faces half green; Albert the left side of his face and Edwin the right side of his, so that they looked like mirror images of each other.

They merged into the gathering crowd, (itself a living kaleidoscope of hundreds of shades of ever-changing green) and joined the back of the queue at the gates. The queue was very slow moving and even though they had tickets they still had to wait at least three quarters of an hour to actually get through the gates. As they waited, Albert turned to his brother and said, "Did you feel as if you were being followed on the way here just then?"

"You mean as we walked from the motel?"

"Yes."

"No. Why?"

"I just got a hunch we were being followed, but each time I turned around, whoever it was had disappeared."

"Oh."

"It's weird. And that's not the only strange thing that's been happening lately."

"Oh?"

"I've been getting strange emails from some 'admirer', now that I'm a widower."

"Really?" Edwin did a double-take. "Don't tell me you're being stalked by some female who's got the hots for you!" Edwin exclaimed, laughing.

"No, I'm serious. It's got to the point now where it's becoming a nuisance. At first, I thought it was a bit of a joke but it's starting to annoy me now. I've definitely been aware of someone following me over the past two weeks. I mean, why pick on me? Why don't they stalk you?"

"Because you're a widower, you're available, you're handsome—you just need to look at me to see that." Then, looking a little dismayed, he said, "But you're not rich, are you? And you don't have a job."

"No. That's what I mean you see. I don't understand. It doesn't make sense."

"The thing is," Edwin said behind his hand to avoid any eavesdropping from bystanders, "you're under suspicion of murder and desecrating a grave. What woman in her right mind would want to associate with you anyway?"

"Exactly."

They took their seats in the grandstand among a sea of supporters with similarly painted faces and colored hair. A pipe band dressed in striking tartan was playing a tune in the arena and this was interspersed with the home team anthem sung in bursts by flag-waving supporters. Irish flags depicting the four provinces almost eclipsed the English Union Jacks. Edwin opened his packet of potato crisps and offered some to Albert. Soon there were loud whistles and cheers and clapping as the two opposing teams strutted onto the field. The match was now on. Ireland scored the first try and mass hysteria broke out in their section of the crowd. Everyone was cheering and whistling and breaking blown up paper bags, except for Albert. Strangely, he had missed seeing that first try.

"Jeez! I bloody missed that! What happened?" he yelled above the din to his brother, who was sitting right next to him.

"Weren't you watching? O'Connell just flew past Fletcher, knocked Webster down and smashed the ball right onto the line. It was awesome!"

"Bugger! Someone just tapped me on the shoulder at the same time and I missed it when I turned around."

"Don't tell me…" Then he mouthed the words, "Miss Nobody?"

Albert nodded.

"Cor blimey!" said Edwin, deliberately turning his attention back to the game. Albert shifted uncomfortably in his seat and grabbed another handful of Edwin's potato crisps. He told himself he must concentrate on the game. He didn't want to miss what he had especially come to see.

Again, there was a roar from the crowd. The other side had just got a penalty. Albert perched on the edge of his seat, determined not to miss anything. The first packet of potato crisps was just about gone. Suddenly, O'Driscoll, Edwin's idol, came bursting out of nowhere with the ball tucked under his arm. He was tearing through the mud and rain straight up the field with no opponents anywhere to be seen. It was going to be a gift, this one. The crowd was right behind him, willing him to dot the ball down between the posts. He did it with ease and just as he drop kicked the conversion, Albert's head inexplicably swung around one hundred and eighty degrees in the opposite direction.

"Jesus! What happened? Did he get it over?" he yelled to his brother.

"Didn't you see that?" Edwin yelled back. "It was perfect. Just perfect. Straight through the posts!"

"Nah! Something's wrong with me bloody neck!" said Albert. He put both hands up to his face and swung his head from side to side. "Should have painted it all green instead of half maybe. I don't know." He sat dejected and gulped from a can of Guinness he had smuggled in. "What the hell is going on?" he asked himself. "I can't even enjoy a game of footy now without something weird happening. I feel like the girl with the swivel-head in *The Exorcist*."

By half-time, there were four tries from the home side and every one that had been converted, Albert missed seeing. Ireland eventually won 49-3 in a complete walkover and all their supporters were elated—doubly so because it was St Patrick's Day. All except Albert. He felt exasperated and elated all at once. In fact, he felt he had been jinxed and cheated of his £25 entrance fee because he had missed the most important parts of the match. As he said to Edwin afterward, "I would have enjoyed the game more if I'd actually seen it."

"Perhaps you're getting the first symptoms of St Vitas' Dance," said Edwin, not very helpfully. "You remember old Mr. McGinty who used to live up the road from us when we were kids? He had that. His head used to go all over the place. Maybe you should see a doctor."

"What? I don't need a doctor. Something weird is happening and I intend to find out what."

*

The after-match party was a mostly male affair in a downtown upstairs flat. The twins could hear the music blaring from the top of the street even before they found a parking spot. They rolled up with plenty of Guinness tucked under their coats to a place packed with all sorts of punk rockers and skinheads with green faces. In fact, they reminded Edwin of a pack of Jumblies (themselves included), whose 'heads were green and hands were blue and they went to sea in a sieve' as in Edward Lear's poem that they used to recite in primary school. Sprinkled among the crowd were a few young women, 'babes' in tight, skimpy mini-skirts and boob tubes, and people snorting what looked like crack and popping party pills. There were rotating colored lights and pulsating psychedelic music. It was mind-blowing.

Albert got stuck into the drink first before his mate Sean came up and introduced him to a girl with billowing red hair who was wearing silver lamé hot pants and a slinky black boob tube. Trudi, who was already half-tanked herself, smiled winningly, put her arm around him and whisked him away to a relatively private corner of the room.

"This one's mine," she said to a girlfriend as they passed.

Albert lapped up all the attention. Maybe this Trudi person could help cheer him up after such a lousy time at the football match. One drink led to another, which led to another and the odd snort of crack or two as well. Albert was finally starting to enjoy himself. Edwin, on the other hand, spread himself around and didn't mix his drinks or take anything suspect. The party went on into the wee small hours, keeping up its momentum as people came and went and as the party pills kept being popped. By now, Albert had flaked out in one of the bedrooms, so Edwin left without him and told Sean he would be back the next morning to pick him up.

But late next morning, when Edwin arrived back at Sean's flat, he was confronted by a different story.

"Albert? Oh, he left about an hour ago. Said he was going downtown to get a tattoo."

"A tattoo?"

"Yeah. He was admiring Trudi's—she had one on her ankle, not on her bum," he snickered. "It was a rose or something. He thought he would go to the same place she went for hers. They're open on Sundays, apparently."

"Whereabouts?"

"Dunno."

"Oh, well, he'll just have to catch the bus home in that case. Silly bugger," said Edwin and took off on his own in Albert's van.

*

By mid-afternoon, Albert and Trudi had gone their separate ways and Albert had got his tattoo. He was now £200 the poorer for it. He was shuffling about through a street full of refuse from the revelry of the night before, feeling slightly seedy and looking for a bus. Impressed on his left shoulder was a tattoo as big as his fist. It said 'Caroline Forever' and was delicately entwined with a Celtic ribbon design. It was partly to absolve himself for what he had got up to the night before and partly to ward off any potential stalkers. He felt as if he had at least some form of protection now, a shield, as it were, against any unforeseen evils. He felt he had done the right thing under the circumstances. It was a tender and fitting tribute to his young now deceased, wife and also it would hold him in good stead with the police. After all, he would hardly have a design like that tattooed on his shoulder if he had murdered her, would he? Albert meandered around Temple Bar's narrow cobbled streets for a while longer, tossing up whether to catch a bus or to just hang out in the park for a time. Peering in through the latticed windows of the various artisans displaying their wares, he decided then to walk along Grafton Street to St Stephen's Green to clear his mind. He recalled the rather appropriate little ditty called 'The Dublin Saunter'.

He went past the statue of Thomas Moore, irreverently placed over the top of a public toilet (now closed) and then strolled past Trinity College on his left. It was a beautiful set of old buildings founded in 1592 by Queen Elizabeth I on the site of an Augustan monastery. Originally a Protestant college, it had only begun to accept Catholics in numbers after 1970 when the Catholic church relaxed its opposition to them attending. Among its many famous students, Albert remembered, were Oliver Goldsmith and Jonathan Swift.

Suddenly Albert stopped in his tracks. Bram Stoker, the author of *Dracula*, was supposed to have studied at Trinity College as well. *How curious,* he thought. He immediately thought of retracing his steps through Temple Bar and crossing the Ha'penny Bridge to visit the crypt at St Michan's Church, north of the Liffey. There, you could actually 'shake hands' with the undead (of sorts). Four macabre mummified bodies were sitting in their open coffins on public display. One of them was said to be eight hundred years old and it was the dry atmospheric conditions of the underground vaults that helped to keep them so well preserved. Albert drew in a quick breath and decided to keep on his present path, as he had had enough of the undead for the time being, all things considered.

He ambled past the wheelbarrowed effigy of Molly Malone, locally known as 'the tart with the cart', until he became inexplicably drawn to Davy Byrne's pub on Duke Street. Memories of that fateful Bloomsday, 16th June 1999 came flooding back as he approached. The pub had been chock-full of people that day and he had been left leaning against a barber's pole next door, dressed in a striped red waistcoat with a battered copy of James Joyce's *Ulysses* under one arm and his straw boater pulled down over his eyes while eating a gorgonzola cheese sandwich with one hand and holding a glass of burgundy in the other. He was waiting for Ed to emerge from the pub with similar fare when a gust of wind blew his hat off to reveal his ponytail at the nape of his neck. Suddenly, Caroline had appeared, peering up at him over the brim of the retrieved hat like some miscreant schoolgirl. Their eyes had met and it was instant attraction. He thanked her for the return of the hat and then, with his tongue unleashed from the drink, asked for her phone number. She obliged (as Neville was nowhere to be seen, having disappeared into the depths of the pub for a couple of souvenir pints while she waited outside). From then on, everything was history, as Albert had followed Caroline back to Abbotts Bromley soon after.

Albert mulled over that rather special day of twenty-one months ago in his mind. He could remember it perfectly. He and Edwin had decided to give Dublin a whirl that day by joining in the spirit of Bloomsday and reliving the life of Leopold Bloom, the lead character in *Ulysses*. The day of 16th June 1914 was an epic voyage of discovery around the streets of Dublin. In similar vein, Albert and Edwin had started off together at six o'clock in the morning with a dip in the *'snotgreen scrotumtightening sea'*, to quote Joyce, before partaking of the obligatory entrails (deep fried kidneys) washed down with a glass of Guinness for breakfast at the Southbank Restaurant.

They had then proceeded on their odyssey to 7 Eccles Street, the now-demolished home of Leopold and Molly Bloom, and on to St George's Church in Hardwicke Place (now converted into an entertainment venue and nightclub), through to Harrison's Restaurant in Westmoreland Street for roly-poly jam puffs—just as Bloom had done in 1914 in the book.

Then it was through to Trinity College to Provost Salmon's statue (not in the original odyssey but now an integral part since its erection). George Salmon was provost of Trinity College from 1888 to 1904. When it was proposed that women be allowed to study there in 1904, he was reputed to have said, "Over my dead body!" His wish was fulfilled prematurely because before the year was out, he was dead and the college accepted its first female students. His prescience had obviously come back to haunt him.

The twins had then gone down through Grafton Street to Davy Byrne's for lunch, where Albert had met Caroline while waiting for Edwin to join him in a bite to eat. After that pleasant little interlude, the brothers had continued on to Oscar Wilde's childhood home in Merrion Square and through to Sweny's Chemist to buy lemon soap à la Molly Bloom.

Interspersed between all this was their spontaneous soliloquizing on street corners to anyone willing to listen to their slightly inebriated impromptu renditions of Joyce's script. There were street performers, fire-eaters, jugglers, stilt-walkers, jazz bands and various actors hamming it up all over town. Finally in the afternoon, they had had a pint together at the Ormond Hotel where both Bloom and Edwin were tempted by barmaids. Albert smiled ruefully at the recollection. It had been a long afternoon…

Noticing that Davy Byrne's was open, Albert went in on an impulse for a quick pint for old time's sake. The pub was just as he remembered it back then, with all its plush décor, only it was less well-patronized this time. There were the same memorabilia on the walls, the same atmosphere of conviviality, but fewer allusions to literary wit and fewer aspirations to it. It was just quieter and more genteel than on that particular Bloomsday when people had been spilling out of the pub and onto the street.

Albert asked for a pint at the bar and raised the black liquid to his lips, savoring the malty taste and creamy froth. Just what he needed…a hair of the dog after the night before. *That was a blast, that party,* he thought. Was he going to make it back to Londonderry that night? He wasn't sure. He still wanted to visit St Stephen's Green and hang out there for a while. He needed to reflect on the nature of his tattoo and the memory of Caroline before anything. He finished his Guinness with one last appreciative swig and placed his glass carefully back on the bar. He studied the empty glass absentmindedly, then thanked the barman and left.

Albert soon reached St Stephen's Green North, formerly known as 'Beaux Walk' in the nineteenth century and still the home of several gentlemen's clubs. He wandered onto the green past the bandstand, lake and fountain, and stood in front of the massive monument to the eighteenth-century nationalist leader, Wolfe Tone, locally known as 'Tonehenge'. *Quite an apt nickname,* he thought, for those who were of the pagan persuasion. Not that Wolfe Tone was a pagan because he was actually a Protestant helping the nationalist cause.

As he wandered through the beautiful grounds, he noticed among the groups of students lying on the grass studying, a nearby outdoor painting exhibition under a group of trees. Curious, he went closer to investigate. He discovered that the paintings were obviously executed by a bunch of very good amateurs. They were not outstanding paintings, but what he would call 'adequate'. He considered himself a harsh critic. Not that he was an expert— far from it, but in his opinion, this was the sort of exhibition that someone like Neville Yelavich might perhaps exhibit at. He had heard in passing from Victor that Neville was an amateur artist of some outstanding talent. He immediately dismissed the idea as being ludicrous and lost all interest in the display. But what else could you expect from a rival in love?

Somewhat miffed, he threw a couple of stones into the calm waters of the lake and then sat down to watch the ripples disperse. He had dispatched Neville

Yelavich and now all he had to do was shake off this damn stalker, whoever she was. And what a waste of £25 at that rugby match! He had to get to the bottom of this. He spent an hour in morbid contemplation and then realized he had a bus to catch. What the heck. It was probably too late now anyway. He would find digs for the night and catch a bus first thing in the morning. Firstly however, he had better phone Davinia about babysitting Dudley for an extra night.

*

He arrived home in Londonderry the next day around lunchtime to the familiar sight of the Maiden City's elegant St Columb's Cathedral spire which dominated the city. Albert lived in the Protestant Fountain area which suited him now as he was a lapsed Catholic and in reality, a neo-pagan. He always felt uncomfortable and conspicuous if he ever needed to visit the Catholic Bogside area for any reason. So much for the 'troubles' now supposed to be over and the sign on the Bogside gable proclaiming, 'You are now entering Free Derry'.

Albert went straight to his den to check if there was any email on his second-hand computer. There were two messages. One was from his brother and it read, '*What the hell do you want a bloody tattoo for?*' The other message was from the stalker, and it said, '*Albert—forever mine. Never Caroline's.*'

Albert was flummoxed. He immediately phoned an internet security firm and a few days later they came back with the report: 'Untraceable' and 'no such phone number'. Albert was worried. Later that day when he picked up Dudley from Davinia's nearby, he decided to confide in her. Davinia had just got off the phone from talking to her latest love interest when Albert arrived at the door.

"See you, honey, bye. Oh, hello, Albert. I didn't see you at the door. Come in."

"Hi, Davinia. I've just come by to collect Dudley. How's he been? A good little trooper?"

"He's been very good, haven't you, Dudley? Such a good boy! So, how are you? Bearing up? I don't suppose you've heard the rumors going around about me and you? We're supposed to be having an affair. Very convenient, living just around the corner from each other, isn't it? That's why you killed your wife apparently. That's according to what I heard from Darryn just now, anyway."

"For God's sake! It's never-ending, isn't it? I've been getting weird emails too from some lovesick cow."

"Well, they weren't from me!"

"Perish the thought! It's time to look up the books again in my library, I think. There's definitely something very fishy going on. And my neck's giving me gyp too. Ed reckons I've got 'symphitis dance', whatever that is. I missed the most important bits of yesterday's match because of it."

"We won that."

"So, I heard," he said. "So, I heard. But it cost me £25 to find out!"

14

Six weeks later, a man was fishing in the River Inny, so named after the mythical Princess Erithne, who drowned and was cremated downstream of Abbeyshrule. The man had just snagged something big from a nearby bog. He had been fishing for pike and when he reeled in this big one. He was almost tempted to cut it free because it was bound to be over the three-kilogram limit, to be sure. He grappled with the fish through the weed and was surprised to find when he brought it to the surface that it wasn't a monster fish after all, but a huge black polythene parcel. He slit it open with his fishing knife and found that it contained two shovels, two pairs of boots, two pairs of gloves, and two parkas. Scratching his head, he unhooked his line and left the package open to the elements before hauling in his legal quota of several salmon and one pike. The unobjectionable-looking package was left in the meantime, singularly abandoned on the riverbank.

When the police finally got wind of this, they immediately put in a request with the forensic department for DNA testing against Neville Yelavich's remains. It would take at least six weeks to process the results. In the meantime, the Pengally twins were still on the police records as prime suspects in the Yelavich staking case and Albert also for the possible homicide of his wife. It was now coming up to Beltane, 1st May, another major Wiccan sabbat and the celebration of the beginning of the Celtic summer. Edwin and Alison had invited Albert and Dudley to spend May Day with them in Letterkenny and to share some Beltane cakes that Alison had especially baked for Albert's benefit. Being a good Wiccan who religiously observed the four major sabbats of the year, Albert readily agreed. They enjoyed an elevenses of fresh cakes before deciding on a short drive out to Kilmacrenan, where there was to be a fair held and a maypole dance that afternoon.

Fortunately, at Kilmacrenan there was a holy well that Alison particularly wanted to visit, so once they had parked the car at a picnic spot and had had lunch, Alison reached for her water bottle and excused herself. She had always been intrigued by the Holy Well of Doon and was now going to exercise her rights. The particular advantage of the water from this well was that it was supposed to be an infallible remedy against infidelity in husbands. She wasn't sure if that included de facto ones, but was willing to give it a try. *There is no harm in taking precautions,* she thought, and filled her water bottle with relish. She returned to the others at the picnic site looking very pleased with herself and raised her water bottle in the air.

"This isn't for human consumption," she announced. "It's going straight on the floor under the bed at home!"

"Oh!" said Edwin, wondering what he had let himself in for. Being a pagan, however, he thought he should have no worries in that direction, even though Alison was a Catholic. They would just have to see how things turned out, just like in any other type of marriage.

Alison grinned. She enjoyed needling him sometimes and putting him on the spot. It gave her a sense of power, even if somewhat displaced.

"Tell you what boys," she said. "I just had a sip of that well water and if you want to know how I am, I'm Doon Well!"

"Oh, very clever," said Albert. "You don't happen to have O'Donnell blood in your veins, do you?"

"No, why?"

"The O'Donnells were inaugurated on Doon Rock, and they're still Doon Well after four centuries."

"Well, there you are, then. It has to be the real thing. But it's a pity I can't hold such a high pedigree to my own name."

"But you're a Fitzherbert," said Albert. "Just don't marry a Fitzhisbert, or your kids won't know if they're Arthur or Martha."

Alison gave Edwin a furtive sideways glance. *Not much chance of that happening,* she thought, *if she keep the water bottle under the bed.*

"Er, no…" she faltered and changed the subject.

By the end of the day, the foursome had been on the merry-go-round at the Kilmacrenan fair, the Ferris wheel, the go-carts, fired shots at moving targets, showed Dudley the baby farm animals and eaten far too many hot dogs. So many hot dogs in fact, that they almost couldn't make it around the maypole. On the way back to Letterkenny, Albert announced in the car that he intended to take Dudley mushrooming under the Hill of Old Oak Trees (the Croic na Coille) on the Ballyliffen Road and then visit Glengad Head the next day.

"Oh, that'll be nice," said Alison, "but it's near the end of the season for mushrooms just now, isn't it?"

"Yes, I suppose so," said Albert, "but it's a good excuse for a walk in an unspoiled area of the country with natural forest."

"I'll tell you about a great unspoiled spot," said Edwin. "Alison and I visited the Poisoned Glen a couple of weeks ago didn't we Alison?"

"Yes, and it was great. So close to home too."

"But the water there is undrinkable," said Edwin, "and there's absolutely no bird life. It's the poisonous sap from all the surge that grows there that's the culprit. And they say that the ruined church in the glen there is haunted. But those ice-carved cliffs are amazing. I got some great shots of the sky reflecting pink off the granite cliff faces after the rain. It'll be just as nice at this time of the year on the peninsula. Don't get lost though. The roads up there might be a bit rugged in places for a pram."

"No worries, mate. We'll cope, won't we Dudley?" he said, poking Dudley in the stomach. "There's nothing we two like more than a bit of a challenge."

*

The next day back in Londonderry, Albert packed some egg sandwiches, drinks and baby food and put the pram in the van. He fastened Dudley into his baby harness and set off for the north western part of the Inishowen Peninsula. On the way, they visited the Grianan of Aileach, originally an ancient pagan temple at the entrance of the peninsula and took in the view of Lough Swilly and Lough Foyle on either side. From here, they could see the sprawling countryside beyond changing color from pastel green to pastel purple as the light played tricks on the misty clouds above. They drove through the seaside town of Buncrana toward Carndonagh, noticing several small wayside shrines as they went. Each shrine depicted the virgin Mary swathed in rosary beads and surrounded by specially picked flowers. Some of these stone pageantries appeared to be making a silent plea for the second coming of Christ.

Heather purpled the valley slopes and in the distance the sky allowed a shaft of light through a moving keyhole of thick cloud to spotlight a gnarled cliff here or there rising from the sea. They passed trim hedges and wan limestone walls bordering smallholdings of sheep and cows, while isolated farmhouses nestled in clumps of sycamore.

Before long, they reached the Hill of the Old Oak Trees on Ballyliffen Road. It was a beautiful unspoiled and lonely spot covered in oak trees, birch, rowan, hazel, and holly. Albert knew there was also a large stone altar or Mass Rock somewhere in the wood where Mass used to be offered in Penal times. Not that he would be looking for it in particular—just a few mushrooms would suffice.

There was not a breath of wind and only a light drizzle that hung like a fine mist in the air. A lone seagull soared high above them and Albert wound down his window and appreciatively breathed in the damp sea air. It was full of all those negative ions, so good for restoring positive thoughts. Getting back to nature was his way of coping with all of life's little stresses. He parked the van by the roadside and then felt inspired to take Dudley for a walk in his pram through the long grass to where a grove of ancient oak trees stood. A lone hawthorn in full blossom by the roadside welcomed them with the promise of spring as they passed.

It was a long walk, but good for the constitution. Dudley was sitting up all alert in his pram and taking an obvious interest in his surroundings. The ground was a bit bumpy, but neither of them seemed to mind. When they arrived at the grove of old oak trees, Albert removed his raincoat and turned it inside out before putting git back on again. It was just a precautionary measure to neutralize any fairy effects there.

"*You can't be too careful in a place like this*," he thought.

Before long, he spied some toadstools standing proud in the long grass. On closer inspection, he realized that this was a fairy ring. These rings could last intact for hundreds of years and just stepping into one could drastically change a person's luck, especially if they were a witch. He decided therefore to leave it well alone and felt glad he had taken protective steps with his coat.

He rambled on with Dudley in the pram and was suddenly struck by a thought. Dew gathered from fairy rings was supposed to work as a love potion for young women. Vaguely, he wondered if his now dead young wife may have ever made use of this piece of little-known Wiccan knowledge. He doubted it, as she had only just begun to take an interest in it in the weeks leading up to her death. He had noticed however, that just before she died, she had been reading Keats's poem about St Agnes, as his father's old volume had been bookmarked at that particular page.

"St Agnes Eve had just passed when she died," he mused. "Surely, she hadn't been deliberately trying to attract another lover? But she hadn't gone 'supperless to bed' that night because of the food poisoning they found with those oysters she'd eaten. Perhaps on the actual night she went supperless to bed. She did seem a lot thinner than usual. But why would she want to attract a dream lover?" Albert pondered the question while Dudley gurgled playfully in his pram. Then he had an idea. "Maybe she really was trying to lose weight over St Agnes Eve, but her plan went badly wrong when it wasn't me who appeared in her dreams, but Neville instead in a nightmare! That's what it was! A spell perhaps that went wrong and attracted her demon lover. But if I remember correctly, all the herbs and candles and essences that she used should have worked. In which case, somehow Neville overpowered her. Poor girl! She didn't stand a chance against such black magic."

He looked sadly at little Dudley, who obviously missed his mother too. It was nearly time for his baby food. Albert looked around for a place to spread the picnic blanket and suddenly spied some brownish, cone-shaped mushrooms, slightly green tinted at the edges and about three inches across.

"Oh, magic mushrooms! Liberty caps! Great! I'll pick some of those."

He left Dudley watching wide-eyed from his pram as he gathered together a good two dozen on them, which he began to eat raw as an entrée before lunch. He ate about ten of these before attempting his egg sandwiches which he had specially brought. He was feeling quite lucky to have found so many of these mushrooms so near to the end of the season.

He fed Dudley his baby food, but then because Dudley put his hand out asking for a mushroom as dessert, Albert complied, but only gave him one. *That would be plenty for a baby,* he thought. As it happened, Dudley merely picked the mushroom to bits, chewed the stalk and spat it out, so he was definitely not getting any more.

Now that they had both eaten, Albert lay back on the picnic rug for a while, watching the ever-changing sky before wheeling Dudley back to the van. He wanted to drive back through Carndonagh to Culdaff and then check out Glengad Head while the weather was still holding.

Thus, father and son soon took off for Glengad Head, not too far away on the north-eastern coast and parked near the summit. It was still misty but strangely enough the wind had dropped, so Albert popped Dudley in the pram and took him for a meander around the clifftops. The cliff views of the churning seas below and the cliff waterfalls were spectacular, although Rathlin Island and Scotland were obscured by cloud and mist. The wreck of the *Alceste*, he knew, was submerged off the coast out there somewhere and had lain there for over a hundred years, together with around another forty or so other wrecks throughout the last couple of hundred years. This place could be quite stormy at times, unlike today. 'Changeable' was the word, just like the Irish temperament, so some liked to say…

Albert pushed the pram further along the clifftop road and then suddenly began to feel a bit strange. It was about an hour after their lunch and the mushrooms were beginning to take effect. With some physical effort, he parked Dudley in his pram safely on the grass verge away from the cliff edge. The psilocybin in the mushrooms was causing both his mood to change and his mental focus. He was beginning to hallucinate. Now he could feel himself floating above the ground and everything was becoming very vivid and surreal to him. He looked down from above and could see himself eating primroses…Horrors! That was supposed to enable you to see fairies! This was quite out of character for him. Confused, he asked himself, "Why am I doing this?"

Suddenly, he seemed to be transported as if into another world. He could hear waves crashing on the rocks below the cliff. Every ninth wave was especially loud. In the background, he could hear a baby crying, but he was mesmerized by the sound of the waves into a state of near paralysis. Then a songbird with an extraordinary voice began singing overhead.

All at once, a beautiful vision appeared before him. Bright quivering lights radiated outward from the vision of a spellbinding goddess who was hovering in mid-air and shimmering before his eyes. She was stunningly beautiful. She had long fair hair and wore a wispy luminous pale sea-green gown with golden cords which crossed over her breasts, Grecian style. She carried a sparkling wand and alighted daintily before him. She was the most beautiful creature he had ever seen.

"Wh…who are you?" he stammered.

"Griselda Yelavich, Neville's sister. Cliodhna to you. I am the Irish goddess of beauty, the sea and the afterlife. I am the fairy queen of Munster and the daughter of Gebran, the last druid of Ireland. Carrig Cliodna is my sacred hill in County Cork. I am the matron of waves, especially every ninth wave that breaks on the seashore. Songbirds and seabirds are my sacred creatures."

"Oh, I've heard of you, Cliodhna. You're beautiful!"

Albert was enchanted.

"Why, thank you, Albert. That is your name, is it not? Yes, of course. Let me show you something," she said.

Then, before you could say 'Jack Robinson'. With one quick tug on her golden cord, her dress fell to the ground and lay about her feet. She stood there glowing splendidly in all her naked glory for Albert to feast his eyes on. Albert's eyes stood out on stalks. He just couldn't help himself. In a flash, he had ripped off all his clothes and was kissing Cliodhna passionately all over her luminous white skin as if all his Christmases had come at once. He allowed himself to become entangled in her yellow hair and to be wooed mercifully by her magic touch. The fiery lustfulness in his loins soon exploded the myth that fairies were unreal. *This* fairy was real flesh and blood! Soon, he was being transported in spasms of unearthly ecstasy to another realm where only mortals and fairies could freely copulate in the copses. Pulses of kaleidoscopic color popped and burst all around him as the power of the magic mushrooms contributed to the hallucinatory effect of his experience. Two birds sang vociferously overhead upon the final climax of their consummated passion and the waves crashed tumultuously upon the seashore below.

"Take me! I'm yours!" he cried, surrendering himself to her.

He lay there bewitched and bewildered, utterly lost to her power. He had become enslaved to this strange sex goddess and was now ripe for being taken away into the underworld with her. Albert was completely under her spell and zombie-like, watched her every move, mesmerized by her utter beauty. Like a child, he pleaded for more, but Cliodhna had other ideas. In complete control, she quickly slipped out of his clutches and put on her robes.

"Get dressed Albert love, and follow me," she said.

Hypnotized, Albert followed obediently three steps behind Cliodhna as she glided over the top of the long grass toward the cliff edge, the hem of her long robes trailing enticingly behind her. When they got to the edge, she turned and smiled enigmatically. She touched him gently on each shoulder with her sparkling wand and then turned and stepped off the cliff, mysteriously vanishing into thin air.

"Follow me," her voice chanted hauntingly as if out of nowhere.

Unable to disobey, Albert inexorably followed and stepped off the cliff. He too mysteriously vanished into thin air…

The only evidence of Cliodhna's visit was the deep depression in the long grass among the copses where they had lain.

Albert the witch was nowhere to be seen. He had been taken away by a fairy to the underworld. It was just as Caroline had foreseen in the black mirror…Albert being overpowered by fairies and surrounded by a fairy ring.

And now Dudley, all alone in his pram, was crying…

15

It was well past dinner time and Ed and Alison were beginning to wonder where Albert and Dudley had got to. Albert had promised to call his brother on the way home with his mushrooms, but had failed to do so. Either he hadn't got any mushrooms, or he was already home, or they had got lost.

"Strange that Albert didn't phone us," said Edwin. "Damn him for not having a cell phone!"

"Perhaps they've gone for a McDonald's," volunteered Alison.

"I doubt it. Albert hates fast food."

By nine o'clock in the evening when Edwin was still unable to make contact with Albert, Ed and Alison were starting to get worried. Albert just wasn't answering his home phone and that was most unlike him. By ten o'clock when there was still no reply, they were thinking that perhaps Albert and Dudley had got lost out on the peninsula. They didn't want to involve the police in particular, so Ed decided that first thing in the morning he would go and look for them.

"I'm coming with you," said Alison. "Have you tried ringing the hospitals?"

"I've done that. No sign of them."

"Blimey. I wonder where they've got to then," said Alison. "Probably got lost somewhere out on the peninsula. It'll be hopeless looking tonight though. We'll just have to start at first light tomorrow."

Ed and Alison left at the crack of dawn the next morning in Ed's car for the north western side of the Inishowen Peninsula where Albert said they were going, and once they arrived at the Hill of Old Oak Trees, they parked the car in a layby at the side of the road. It was raining slightly and a light breeze was wafting the blossom-laden hawthorn tree about at the side of the road.

"Okay, let's just remember," said Ed, "he would have chosen an easy path because he would have been pushing a pram. Let's check out that grove of old oaks over there. There might be mushrooms growing there."

After a good fifteen minutes' walk, they came across a fairly open expanse dotted with a few birch trees and a big grove of old oak trees. The oaks looked as if they had existed for hundreds of years because the trunks were so solid and twisted and gnarled. A light wind rustled all the leaves overhead as if they were whispering secrets to each other, the multi-fingered leaves pointing in all directions at once. It was as if the trees had decided not to tell them anything helpful at all but were leaving them alone to search by themselves.

All at once something caught Alison's eye.

"Look! Mushrooms!" she called out. She pointed to where a collection of liberty caps lay strewn across the ground. "I bet Albert picked those!"

"Mmm, I think you're right," agreed Ed. "They look like those hallucinatory magic mushroom things. Silly bugger. Didn't he know he was playing with fire?"

"Let's take them home," said Alison. "We can get them checked if we need to."

She scooped them up and put them into the fold-up carry-all that she had brought with her specially. Then scanning the ground, they checked to see if they had missed anything such as lunch wrappings or whatever, but they were unable to find any other clues. After spending another hour searching, they gave up and decided to check out Glengad Head.

They were in luck because as soon as they arrived, they spotted Albert's van parked near the summit. Otherwise, the place was deserted except for the occasional whistling of the wind through the wires of the radio mast standing sentinel there. Edwin drew up alongside the van and peered through the windows. There was no sign of the pram and when they checked the doors, they were all securely locked.

"Okay," said Ed, "he's taken the pram. Let's go down this way here and follow this track through the long grass. It looks like he might have taken the pram down through there. It seems to lead over to that cliff edge way over there by the looks of it."

"Okay, I'll follow you," said Alison. In five minutes, they had spotted it.

"Look! There's Dudley's pram!" Alison called out.

They ran over to where the pram was, about a hundred yards away parked on the grass verge and peered in. There was little Dudley, lying limp and exhausted from crying. He needed a good feed too.

"Oh, damn! I forgot to bring any baby food," said Ed.

"Hang on," said Alison. "That looks like their lunch box over there."

She picked up the red plastic lunch box and found two leftover egg sandwiches and a small can of unopened baby food with a tin opener.

"Cripes, the poor little fellow must be starving!" said Alison.

She quickly got to work, opened the can and began spooning food into Dudley's open mouth.

"There, that's better isn't it, Dudley? You were hungry, weren't you? I'll take your nappy off now and wrap you up in your blanket."

She did the honors and then Ed said, "So, where's Albert then? He can't be too far away, can he? Unless he's had an accident…"

He peered around and spied a hollow in the long grass beside a patch of scrub. From here, a set of footprints led off. Curious, he said, "I'm just going to see where these footprints take me, Ally. Won't be too long."

He followed the swathes of long grass that had been swept aside as if someone had made their way toward the cliff edge. He finished up there at the clifftop, overlooking a relatively benign sea with breakers down below. He looked down and felt a slight touch of vertigo. The cliff was sheer and went straight down. A perfect place for a suicide if you were that way inclined. He called out, "Albert! Al…bert!" and listened for a response, but there was nothing. Not even the merest hint of an echo.

"Oh my God, where is the poor guy? I'm starting to feel that something is very wrong."

Shivers ran up his spine and he suddenly felt cold. He had a sudden urge to flee but his manhood demanded that he hold his ground…at least until Alison had witnessed the scene below. He turned around and called out to Alison, motioning her across.

"Follow in my footsteps," he called. "Leave Dudley. He'll be okay."

Alison settled Dudley down in the pram and then went to view Ed's findings.

"Looks like he walked over here to the clifftop," said Ed, "but I can't trace his steps from here at all. He couldn't have fallen because the cliff is really sheer with only a few rocks at the bottom on that little beach. Must be at least three hundred feet high, this cliff. He was wearing that black velvet Akubra hat with the two pheasant feathers in it wasn't he? No bright colors. But I can't even see any trace of a speckled pheasant feather down there."

Suddenly, Ed had another attack of vertigo and had to hang onto his girlfriend.

"No, I can't see any sign of him either," said Alison. "I'd say you could only get down there to that tiny beach by boat anyhow. So, what do we do now?"

"I don't know. I just sense that something really weird has happened. I don't know what it is. Maybe it's a twin thing, call it what you will, but this place makes me feel really creepy. Let's get out of here."

He turned to go, pushing Alison away from the clifftop as he did so.

"Okay. Let's go back home then. I'll take the lunch things if you wheel Dudley back through the long grass," she said.

They arrived back at where Dudley was parked in the pram and wheeled him purposefully back to the summit. Then as quick as lightning, they were back beside the two vehicles, folding up Dudley's pram. Ed drove the van home with Dudley in it and Alison drove Ed's car. They both had the jitters, especially Edwin. He sensed some kind of foul play. It was an uncanny feeling.

*

"What are we going to tell Louise and Victor?" Alison asked when she was changing Dudley into a clean nappy back at their flat. "That Albert has done a midnight flit? Gone into hiding? Gone fishing? Drowned? Been abducted by aliens? Been kidnapped? Been taken by vampires? What do we tell them, Ed?"

"I don't know. Perhaps he was drowned. The tide was out when we were there, so it would have been in last night. Maybe he did fall, knock his head and get washed out to sea. It's possible if he became disorientated after eating those magic mushrooms. They can be almost as strong as LSD if enough of them are eaten. Silly fool. But strangely enough, I just have this feeling that he's still alive somewhere. I don't know why. Maybe it's the twin thing— telepathy if you like. I just sense that he's somewhere else, happy, but not happy. Like he's a prisoner, a prisoner of love even. Cripes, don't ask me why, I just know!"

He stopped and then said with a sense of realization, "Did you know he told me at the big footy match six weeks ago that he felt he was being stalked?"

"No!"

"He said he was getting nuisance emails from some weird woman and that he was being followed by somebody as well. Whenever he turned around, they were gone."

"Strange."

"And then at the footy match he kept missing all the good bits. It was like he was being punished for all the things he enjoyed doing, like watching sport and having loved Caroline. I kidded him that he had a health problem with his neck at the time, but deep down I know there was something more to it."

"Crikey…that's weird."

"I told you he had that tattoo put on his shoulder, didn't I? 'Forever Caroline' it said. Maybe that was the catalyst that just pushed the stalker over the edge to take him away off the cliff. Do I sound like I'm talking sense to you or do you think I'm away with the fairies?"

"Edwin, I know you have had, and always will have a very strong bond with your twin brother…whether he's dead or alive. It's part of being an identical twin. It's ingrained. So, I believe you and what you say about sensing that Albert is still alive somewhere. Perhaps he really was abducted then, especially if he was being stalked. But he's not the type to go somewhere he doesn't want willingly, is he?"

"No. I think he may have been taken willingly, but under false pretenses."

"Oh dear. Poor Albert. In the clutches of some desperate stalker. So, who do you think might be responsible, Ed?" Alison asked.

"Well, Albert is a man with enemies. Enemies in spite of his inherently mild nature. I wouldn't be surprised if that Neville Yelavich were tied up in all this, you know. He would have had a bone to pick with Albert if he were still alive as one of the undead. Albert staked him in the grave you see."

"But Neville is defunct now."

"Yes, but he has relatives, doesn't he? Dead, undead, and alive…"

"Cripes!"

"Vampires are capable of all sorts of atrocities. Their magic is mainly black—Albert's is white. And vampires are capable of shape-shifting too, so that can be *really* misleading. I have a strange feeling that Albert is trying to tell me he's been abducted by some kind of vampire disguised as a woman."

"No! In that case, because you assisted him at the staking, you could be the next victim." Alison looked shocked as she spoke and went very pale.

"And I'm his twin brother…even more incriminating."

"Oh, no, Edwin!"

Alison ran to her boyfriend and held him close.

"Don't worry Ally. If I ever am abducted, I will truly find a way to rescue Albert from whatever prison he's in and make our escape. Good always triumphs over evil in the end you know."

"I hope so Ed," Alison smiled. She picked at the bits of snagged wool on his jersey. "So, what are we going to do Ed?" "What are we going to do with Dudley? We can't keep him here, because we both work. I don't mind looking after him for a few days at a time, but not full-time if I'm going to get anything constructive done with my contract work at home. We'll have to give him to Louise and Victor to look after."

"Yes, that's what I think too. I'll give them a call straight after lunch…once I think of something to say about where Albert's gone."

*

That afternoon, there was a phone call at the Mallorys' in Abbots Bromley.

"I'll get it," said Louise. "Hello?"

"Louise? Oh, this is Ed Pengally, Albert's brother. Albert's gone away for a while and we're not sure when he'll be back. The thing is, he's left Dudley with us, but with us both working, we're not able to look after him full-time. We wondered if you and Victor would like to look after him."

There was absolutely no hesitation on the other end of the line.

"We'd love to! We'd be delighted. When would you like us to take him on?"

"Well, whenever you're able to come over, you can take him straight away."

"Fantastic! What's your address again? Oh, I think we've got it somewhere."

"Twenty-nine Kenty Avenue, Letterkenny, County Donegal."

"That's right, I remember now. I can be there the day after tomorrow," she said.

"Great!"

"So, what's happened to Albert again?"

"Oh, I think he's just been a bit down since Caroline…you know…and he just wants to be alone and travel around by himself a bit, sort of thing. So, we don't know exactly when he'll be back."

"Oh of course. I quite understand. We both miss Caroline too. But it will be wonderful to have Dudley to stay, even for a little while. We'll spoil him rotten, don't you worry!"

Ed laughed. "We've got plenty of supplies of his baby food and nappies and everything, so he'll come pretty well set up."

"Great. Well then, I'll call you as soon as I arrive at the airport in Belfast."

"Lovely. Thanks Louise. Bye."

"Bye."

Louise could hardly contain her excitement as she ran to tell Victor who was busy re-reading the Sunday papers.

"Victor! Guess what? Dudley's coming to stay!"

"Really? That's great news! What about his father?"

"Albert's gone away for a while to sort himself out. Overseas, or somewhere."

"Perfect!"

They hugged each other and decided to celebrate with a nice hot cup of tea and some fancy cupcakes that Louise had just baked that morning. All they needed was a dusting of icing sugar and a blob of cream on each one to make it a perfect ending to the afternoon.

Halfway through his second cupcake, Victor suddenly said, "I've just realized. The police won't like the fact that Albert's gone overseas, will they? They won't like it at all. And I should think that neither will Albert when he gets back."

"That's the risk he takes," said Louise. "I hope he knows what he's doing…"

*

On the day that Louise arrived in Belfast to collect Dudley, she phoned Ed's place from the airport. Alison answered the phone. She sounded terrible.

"Louise? Oh, hello. You're coming to collect Dudley, aren't you?"

"Yes, love. I should be there in around two hours or so."

"Fine. It's just that…we've had some bad news. The police were around here yesterday and arrested Edwin. He's been taken into custody at the police station in Londonderry. The police were able to reconcile some DNA found on the inside of a pair of gloves they discovered recently to the DNA in Neville Yelavich's remains at the morgue in Manchester. They did re-checks on blood samples found in Albert's van too, and found that it all correlated. They also found traces of Neville's blood on our driveway where Albert hosed his van down. And because two people were suspected of desecrating Neville's grave, Ed has been arrested as Albert's accomplice."

"Oh, that's shocking news. What are you going to do?"

"I don't know. I'm under suspicion as well as an accessory for covering up for Albert when he was supposed to be here but was really in Abbots Bromley. I know they're still looking for Albert and they're grilling Ed as to his whereabouts. But we just don't know where he is."

"Oh Alison, I wish I could help. I'll be around as soon as I can. Don't worry, hang in their love. I'll see you soon."

Louise hung up the phone and bit her lower lip.

"Oh glory!" she said to herself. "Looks like Albert's in it up to his neck. I had no idea it would get this bad. And now his brother's been locked up. What will they do with Albert next when he gets back, or is he going to be permanently on the run? Good Lord…I wonder what Victor will say when I tell him. 'I told you so'!"

She hoisted up her shoulder bag and got into the driver's seat of the rental car she had hired. She was driving over the legal speed limit all the way from Belfast and narrowly missed getting a ticket from a patrol car parked just within her range of vision of a straight stretch of country road. She praised God for the car having good brakes.

When she arrived at Ed's flat, Alison was holding Dudley and was in tears. Louise felt guilty about taking Dudley away from her and leaving her all alone in an empty flat. The poor girl looked so distraught that Louise offered to bring Dudley over for a visit as often as she could to keep her company.

"You must phone me Alison, any time you need to. We don't want this family completely falling to pieces. And come over and visit whenever you like too. And bring Ed when he's done his time. That goes for Albert too, if he ever dares to show his face around here. Victor and I really appreciate all you've done in helping to care for Dudley since Carline's been gone. You really have been a rock you know. We don't want you to forget that, love. So, dry your eyes. Just remember, things are always darkest before the dawn."

Alison attempted a half-smile through her tears and kissed Louise and Dudley goodbye. She had become like a second daughter to Louise.

16

Edwin sat on the edge of his bed in his cell and looked at the floor. He couldn't believe the police had moved so quickly. *If only Albert had been a bit more thorough in cleaning out the van and hosing down the driveway,* he thought, *then he wouldn't be sitting in this place staring at these four walls.* He found it incredible that a single molecule of blood could be so incriminating. He had already spoken to his lawyer, Simon Bristow, who told him that if he was proven guilty, he could expect a maximum of five years in jail or three years on parole for good behavior. He also warned that Alison, if proven to be an adjunct to the crime in withholding vital evidence of his whereabouts, could be fined five thousand pounds.

Edwin was full of remorse. He wished he had never become involved in this vampire hunt in the first place. But what could he do? Stand by and watch while a troupe of vampires terrorized his twin brother's family? He thought not. There was more to being a twin than that. They were blood brothers and what one suffered the other must also inherently suffer. He would fight to the death if he had to, to save the soul of his brother.

But he felt trapped. Here he was, starting to rot away in a cold jail cell while his brother was incarcerated God knew where in some dark, dank prison laden down with chains and being supped upon every night and becoming weaker and weaker for all he knew. He had to do something and fast. But what?

He racked his brain. The hearing was in a week's time and the police had put a warrant out for Albert's arrest. Edwin knew they would never find him, not unless he could get to him first. And then if Edwin did find him, Albert would have to go into hiding. If he were found by the police, he could expect to get at least ten years.

Edwin sipped from the glass of water that was beside his bed, deep in thought. If only he could talk to Albert. He focused his mind upon his brother and absentmindedly watched as a cricket crept across the floor waving its antennae at him. It chirped and then jumped onto the bed beside him.

"You're a chirpy little fellow, aren't you?" Edwin remarked.

He had been devoid of visitors for the past two days and so felt the need for conversation, even if only with a lowly insect. The cricket waved its antennae at him again and chirruped in reply, but Edwin soon got tired of watching the cricket's antics. He was tired from racking his brain all day and before long the incessant background music of the lone cricket's song sent him off into a profound sleep.

Soon he was snoring softly in time with the cricket's song and dreaming of somewhere far, far away. He was standing on a cliff edge somewhere and he could see rainbows in the mist. There were four rainbows, to the north, south, east and west. He had never seen anything like it before. Did that mean there were four crocks of gold out there? Just where was he exactly?

Suddenly, out of nowhere, a beautiful woman surrounded by a glowing light and wearing diaphanous robes materialized before him. He gasped in amazement.

"Do not be afraid, Edwin," said the vision. "I am Cliodhna, the Irish goddess of beauty, the sea, and the afterlife."

"Oh…oh…!" Edwin stuttered.

"I hear you're looking for your brother. Is that correct?"

"Yes."

"Then I can take you to him if you wish," she said in her beguiling voice. "Follow me…"

She turned and indicated with her wand for him to follow her off the cliff edge.

"Have no fear," she said. "You will not fall while I am here with you. You are under my protection."

Edwin obediently did as he was bid, but as he got closer to the cliff edge, something made him reconsider.

"Why do you hesitate?" asked Cliodhna. "You will not fall."

"It's not that. It's just that I…er…" Edwin faltered.

He had suddenly become suspicious of this strange and compelling woman. *What if she were an impostor or a shapeshifter,* he thought. She could be attempting to abduct him to the underworld for all he knew. Cliodhna became impatient.

"I demand that you follow me!"

Still Edwin didn't budge.

"Very well then," she said, countering his inaction by slowly and calculatingly disrobing in front of him, watching him intently as she did so.

"There!" she said.

She stood completely naked before him; her pale skin gleaming like polished alabaster. She was as perfect as the Venus de Milo. Then to make her point absolutely clear, she tossed her head back and began moaning faintly.

Edwin held his ground. He would not be swayed. Every fiber in his very being was fighting against what his brain was telling him. Sweat began to run off his brow and his whole body began trembling uncontrollably. But still he made no approach. Cliodhna was starting to get a bit huffy. Suddenly she snapped,

"What's the matter man? Are you gay?" Then snickering she said, "Or impotent?"

Edwin kept silent for a moment and considered his answer.

"Neither."

"Well, I have never been so insulted in all my life. You older twins are all the same. As stubborn as they come. You are the older twin, aren't you? By half an hour I believe. I know things you see." Then becoming impatient once more she snarled, "Young man, if you do not come to me this instant, I will have no alternative but to…"

Edwin cleared his throat in nervous anticipation.

"…set Bruno onto you," she said, lashing out with her wand.

"Wha…?" said Edwin.

But it was too late. In a flash, she was gone and, in her place, stood a huge rottweiler with almighty jaws, champing at the bit and pawing the ground. "Sick him, Bruno!" said a cackling voice from out of nowhere.

Edwin writhed on his bed as he struggled with the savage brute full of demons. His bedclothes flew everywhere and he beat the air with his fists. In five minutes, it was over. He didn't stand a chance. Edwin lay completely still and immobile. Blood began to seep into the sheets.

*

All through the night, everything remained deathly still and silent. Nothing could disturb the sleep of the dead. Then at first light, there was the jangling of keys as the jailer on the morning shift did his rounds. The sound grew louder as he approached Edwin's cell. "Holy smoke!" the jailer cried. "What the hell's been going on here?"

He raised the alarm and soon two or three other officials stood looking in on Edwin's body and the scene of his attack. Someone whistled in amazement and another scratched his head.

"Did you see or hear anything on the TV monitor last night, Jefferson?"

"Nope. Not a thing. Didn't get a peep out of it."

"Crikey. The poor guy looks like he's been half eaten alive. Look at those teeth marks! What do you make of that? Animal bites of some sort I'd say. Nobody came visiting with a pit bull terrier yesterday, did they?"

"Nope. This guy wasn't allowed visitors anyway until the hearing next week."

"Well, something's had a go at him good and proper. There's blood all over the place. We'll have to get a doctor to look at him."

Shortly afterward, the doctor arrived in his white coat. He was a short bespectacled man whose coat barely did up at the front. If Caroline were still alive, she would have recommended the herbal tea and grapefruit diet to him. Dr Shand adjusted his spectacles and felt for a pulse. Then he shone a light into Edwin's pupils and examined the lacerations on his head, neck, limbs and torso. When he had finished, he stood up and pronounced, "Death would have occurred approximately eight hours ago at about 11 pm, I would say. This gentleman has a broken neck, deep lacerations all over his body and a puncture mark on his neck. Once his neck was broken, death would have been instant."

Another doctor was called in for a second opinion later in the day. After much deliberation, the two doctors agreed that the puncture mark was probably from a bite by a vampire bat and the lacerations from some kind of animal such as a pit bull terrier. These findings still had to be confirmed by the zoologist from London Zoo and by a couple of local vets.

In the meantime, the scene of the attack and Edwin's body were sealed off from the rest of the prison while detectives continued looking for any further clues about the mayhem that had gone on unseen and unheard the night before. The night watchmen were interviewed, the security guards, the evening visitors, and the TV surveillance men. They were convinced that someone must have seen or heard something. After all, this brutal attack had taken place within the hallowed walls of the prison itself, where law and order is supposed to be enforced twenty-four hours a day. What kind of idiot would be stupid enough to commit murder right under the very noses of the police and then think they could get away with it?

Edwin's next of kin was notified, this now being his de facto wife, Alison, as his parents were dead and his twin brother was still untraceable. A couple of policewomen were sent around to tell her the bad news.

"Alison Pengally?"

"Yes, I'm Edwin's de facto wife."

"Sergeant McGovern and Sergeant Cronin. Bad news, I'm afraid. May we come in?"

Alison grew pale and showed them both into the lounge where they all sat down.

"I'm sorry," said Sergeant McGovern, "but Edwin has been found dead in his cell."

"What?"

That was the last thing Alison needed to hear.

"I'm sorry. It's been a shock to us all. This type of incident is not the sort of thing you expect to hear when a person is supposedly safely locked away in police custody. We are investigating the incident. It seems to have been some sort of dog attack, although a different type of bite was also found on his neck, possibly a bat bite. We hope to get to the bottom of this as soon as possible because of course, this type of incident is of extreme embarrassment to the police. And not only you, but all of us would like to know who is responsible."

Alison was numb with shock. "Do you have any family nearby? We can offer you victim support if you need it."

"Oh no, thank you. My family lives in Australia and Ed's twin brother's in-laws live in Abbots Bromley in Staffordshire."

"Right. Well, if you need anybody to help you over this sudden loss, I'll give you my card," said Sergeant McGovern. "We're here to help, especially at times like this."

"Thank you."

Alison showed the two policewomen to the door in a daze. As if on automatic pilot, she made herself a cup of tea and then phoned Louise.

Louise stood stock still in shocked disbelief.

"I don't believe it," she said. "Who would do a thing like that to a poor defenseless man locked up in a prison cell? It's madness. Who would do such a thing?"

"I don't know," sniffed Alison.

"Well, I'll tell you what love, I'll come over tomorrow and keep you company. I'll bring Dudley. Victor can fend for himself for a while."

*

Meanwhile, back at the prison they found that there had been a hitch in the surveillance system. It had happened between 11 and 11.30 pm the previous night, so they had no record of what was happening to Edwin in his cell at that time. The videotape was blank and the sound system had automatically switched off simultaneously. The surveillance men had been grilled intensely, but there was no explicable cause for the hitch. The police were flummoxed. They searched throughout the day for fingerprints and any other clues that might happen to show up, all the while feeling quite numb with embarrassment.

17

Edwin's funeral was a simple affair. He was of a similar persuasion to his brother, Albert, although more of a generic neo-pagan than a fully-fledged Wiccan. At his funeral, Alison had arranged for some late-flowering daffodils and jonquils to be displayed in the same little chapel where Albert had originally intended Caroline's funeral to be held, out toward Malin Head on the Inishowen Peninsula. Instead of being cremated however, Alison had arranged for him to be buried, as Albert was still not around to arrange otherwise. The yellow and white flowers added a hint of last Easter to the occasion for those who were so inclined. Songs from Sinead O'Connor's latest CD were played and May Fry's poem was recited by the funeral celebrant.

Do not stand at my grave and weep.
I am not there, I do not sleep.
I am a thousand winds that blow,
I am the diamond glints on snow.
I am the sunlight on ripened grain.
I am the gentle autumn rain.
When you waken in the morning's hush
I am the swift, uplifting rush
Of quiet birds in circled flight.
I am the soft stars that shine at night.
Do not stand at my grave and cry;
I am not there. I did not die.

The poem was so beautiful that not only Alison and Louise but a lot of the congregation, small though it was, wept openly. They were all still coming to terms with Edwin's sudden death. Another young person had been cruelly taken from them.

Edwin's death had been so unexpected and yet coincidental as well because Edwin's sister-in-law, Caroline, had also recently suffered a sudden and traumatic death. She too, had a puncture mark on her neck. The only difference was that Caroline also showed bruises and evidence of drowning, whereas Edwin suffered lacerations. The puncture marks in both cases had been proven to be from vampire bats, their droppings having been found at the scene of Caroline's death, but not at Edwin's. The cause of Caroline's bruises had not yet been ascertained exactly, but Edwin's lacerations were definitely found to be caused by dog bites.

However, the method of entry into Edwin's cell was still a puzzle to police. If only their videotape had been working properly that night. They had thought of it being a possible inside job but, as yet, could not pin down anyone for a motive. What was the point of killing a convicted man?

It looked to them more like some form of ritual vindictive killing, like some sort of tit-for-tat thing. They had even gone so far as to interview Mr. Yelavich senior back in Abbots Bromley in case there was a connection there—Edwin having helped in Neville Yelavich's grave desecration—but so far, they had drawn a blank.

The Yelavichs were definitely under suspicion however, especially since Neville's body when exhumed, was proved to have been staked like that of a vampire by the Pengally twins—or rather, by Albert, as he was the twin with the greater motive, his deceased wife having once been Neville's fiancée. The chief inspector found himself thinking that if this feud between the Yelavich family and the Pengally/Mallory clan didn't stop soon, there would be no one left. It seemed to him to be a case of the vampire faction versus the neo-pagan faction, but just which one was going to win—the followers of Cernunnos, 'the Horned One', or the followers of the Vampyre cult?

They had yet to find out.

One thing that did leave the chief inspector a little disturbed, however, was just who was responsible for the ransacking and burning of the Mallorys' house? They had still found no evidence, which made him wonder if this was another tit-for-tat payback for something that had already happened…like Neville Yelavich's death, perhaps. Victor Mallory was the killer in that first instance, even though it was a so-called accident. Did this mean then, that Neville Yelavich was avenging himself in the undead form by ransacking their house?

The chief inspector shuddered at the thought…

18

Two years later Albert had still not shown up. Louise and Victor and their adopted daughter-in-law, Alison, had not given up hope however. Every 10th May, they observed his disappearance with a day of remembrance together. Even Victor joined in reminiscing about his Wiccan ways and how alien they were to him. He could accept now that although the two of them had been different, they were still family. He had learned to become more tolerant in his old age.

Dudley was flourishing in the care of his grandparents and relishing all the love and attention lavished on him. He was growing up fast, had finished teething and crawling and had just begun talking in sentences. In fact, he was becoming quite mobile now and Louise was finding she was having to keep an eye on him almost constantly. He was becoming quite a handful, getting his hands into everything, make-up included—and not only Louise's, but Victor's as well! Victor was not amused.

Victor and Louise were still happy in their rented apartment in spite of the fact that it was a little small now with a baby around the place, but they would rather have had Dudley there than not. He was their little piece of Caroline after all, and someone to remember her by.

Dudley's third birthday on April 3rd was coming up in a few days' time and Louise had invited Alison, and Davinia and Liam from Ireland and all Dudley's kindergarten friends, together with their mothers, to a birthday lunch. It was to be a fancy-dress party. Dudley was getting excited because it was to be his first real birthday party with guests. There was going to be ice cream and jelly, chocolate cake, little cupcakes iced with hundreds and thousands, butterfly cakes, peanut butter and honey sandwiches, lots of lollies, streamers, balloons, party hats and paper whistles.

The day soon dawned and the first of the arrivals turned up at 11 am. They came as pixies, elves, ET, Little Hot Stuff, Alice in Wonderland, Miss Piggy,

Donald Duck, Peter Pan, Brer Rabbit, Mary Mouse and a brick from the Three Little Pigs' house. Dudley himself was dressed as an angel. He insisted on wearing a pair of wings, but it took quite a lot of convincing from Victor to talk him into being an angel rather than a fairy.

Once everyone had arrived, they all crammed into the lounge which had doors extending into the dining room. A trestle table had been laid with serviettes and goodies and the little children tucked in, all fingers and thumbs, soon demolishing everything in sight. Bibs had to be changed and mouths and noses wiped at various intervals, while the Teletubbies played on the TV in the background.

Soon it was time for the birthday cake and to blow out the candles. Dudley sat down with much aplomb in front of the cake and took a deep breath. He blew out all three candles in one breath. Everyone cheered and clapped and sang 'Happy Birthday' while Dudley basked in all the glory. The cake was cut and then all was relatively quiet again as the children began to eat.

"Hasn't Dudley grown lately?" Davinia remarked in the interval. "How tall is he now, Louise?"

"Thirty-eight inches, which is three foot two. I just measured him yesterday. Yes, I think he's going to be as tall as Victor when he grows up. Maybe even taller."

"He's so much like Victor, isn't he? It's the nose I think, don't you?"

"Yes. Caroline had the same nose, too, but the mouth is more like Albert's, I think. He doesn't take after me at all. Unless he wants to be a ballet dancer when he grows up!"

"I think he's more likely to be a body builder," said Victor. "He's a little toughie, really."

"Yes, maybe even a Morris dancer, dear. We'll have to wait and see, won't we?"

There was a pause and then Alison said, "He might even want to become a witch like his father. Poor little orphan."

All the mothers stared at Alison aghast.

"Oh, it's all right," said Alison. "There's nothing wrong with being a witch. There's nothing spooky about it or anything. It's a form of paganism. Pagans regard the whole universe as divine and regard life as an endless cycle of death and rebirth. It's not a patriarchal religion like Christianity or Islam or Judaism, but a religion of nature. And Wicca is just an occult form of paganism."

The mothers all shifted uncomfortably in their seats and Louise looked disconcertedly across from Alison to Victor and back. Dudley threw his head back and stuffed more birthday cake into his mouth with both hands.

Alison was not to be stopped.

"I'm sure Albert wouldn't mind if Dudley becomes a witch when he grows up…if he comes back in time to actually see Dudley grow up that is."

A murmur of disapproval went around the room as all the mothers tut-tutted about Albert not coming back to shoulder his parental duties and instead dumping the burden on Dudley's grandparents. Louise caught Alison's eye and put a cautionary finger to her lips. Alison shrugged nonchalantly in response.

Then changing the subject, Louise announced somewhat expansively, "I'd just like everyone here to know that it has been an absolute pleasure to have little Dudley stay with us these past almost two and a half years. He is the dearest little fellow—most of the time—and I'm sure Victor would agree when I say we wouldn't mind if he stayed with us forever…or at least until he decides to leave of his own accord. We don't really mind what he decides to do later in life, as long as he is healthy and happy and does no-one any wrong. So, let's raise our glasses everyone and drink a toast to Dudley's future."

The grown-ups all sipped their tea or soft drink and chanted as one, "To Dudley's future."

The party continued with more helpings of birthday cake, bursting of balloons, tweeting of paper whistles, pulling-off of paper hats, smearing of little faces and crumbling of food by little fists held over plates. Dudley grimly held onto his wired-on halo as Little Hot Stuff tried to steal it from him. "Let me have it," said the little boy in the red suit.

"No! Mine! Mine!" retorted Dudley, pulling away.

"Now then you two," said Little Hot Stuff's mother. "That's sacrilege, Tommy. Hands off!" and she gently slapped his hand. His face crinkled into a scowl and then he screwed up his face some more and yowled a voluminous yowl.

"Me want! Me want!" he bellowed vociferously.

"No dear. Leave Dudley alone. You don't want his halo. Look, what about your horns? There's a good boy. Have another piece of birthday cake. That's better."

The matter now resolved; Dudley began playing the drums on his plate with two teaspoons. His smeary face became covered in a huge grin. He was enjoying not only the noise he was making and its staccato rhythm, but also the power he held in subjugating everyone else to his capriciousness. This went on for a good five minutes while the tolerance of the adults was tested and thankfully Little Hot Stuff managed to whip one of the spoons out of Dudley's hands. This he put to his own use on his own full plate, with much more mess but much less racket.

After lunch, there were games for all the littlies with Victor in charge. First there was a lolly scramble, then musical chairs, hide and seek and then a story. Victor was enjoying himself because he was just a big kid at heart. In fact, he would have made a superb Santa Claus at Christmastime. The kids were just eating out of his hands and they loved his story about the Three Billy Goats Gruff when he acted out the part of the old troll. They all squealed with delight when he said he was coming out from under the bridge to eat them all up.

Later Dudley opened all his presents and the children amused themselves playing with these while all the mothers did the washing up in the kitchen. Among Dudley's presents were a jigsaw puzzle, a huge plastic multicolored beach ball, a gigantic teddy bear, a plastic tip truck, a mouth organ and a bag of bubble gum. Dudley was experimenting with his new mouth organ when Victor noticed that his angel wings had come adrift.

"Here Dudley. Let me fix your wings. You're falling to bits," he said.

Dudley obediently went over to his grandfather with the wings in his hand and turned around. Victor knelt down and when he had finished pinning the wings back on said, "Turn around again and let me look at you Dudley. That's it. You look great!"

Then still kneeling, he reached around and adjusted the wings once more, holding them out wide across his back. Dudley stood looking at him with his finger in his mouth.

"Just remember, Dudley," Victor said, "little boys can do anything; play dress-up, do ballet, or body building or Morris dancing, or even be a witch or maybe even a fairy when they grow up. Can't they love?" he said, winking at Louise, who had just emerged from the kitchen.

"Yes dear. Anything they want," said Louise, raising an eyebrow.

Dudley regarded them both with some skepticism. "Just as long as you don't do anything stupid and take after your mother's ex-fiancé. He was a real enigma. Who would have expected him to be a modern-day vampire?" Victor asked rhetorically.

Dudley stared at him and gurgled. Unexpectedly, he burped and a trickle of raspberry cordial ran obliquely down from the corner of his mouth. He smiled roguishly through his baby teeth and his eyes began to glow like hot coals.

Victor stared at him in disbelief. Suddenly, a horrific realization struck. Could this baby boy be Neville Yelavich's offspring? Surely not! He looked more like a Pengally than a Yelavich to him, but then again, look at those eyes! Was he imagining things, or was he just now beginning to feel faint? He steadied himself with some effort, but seemed hypnotized for the moment and could not shift his gaze. This young boy, this small piece of Caroline, his own flesh and blood…surely…(he could not bear to think it) surely, he could not be a vampire. That would make him, Victor, a vampire's grandfather*! Horrors!*

His attention was momentarily diverted when Louise called out from the kitchen, "More raspberry drink, anyone?"

Victor looked at Dudley again. Was this why Caroline had jilted Neville two weeks before their intended wedding? Had she known of Neville's true identity? But was she already with child at the time? He would never know. At least until Dudley had grown out of his baby teeth…

<h1 style="text-align:center">19</h1>

Some sixty years later, long after the Yelavich staking case had hit the headlines, there was to be an auction held in the Manchester Art Gallery. An anonymous donor had brought in a nude painting for auction to raise funds for charity. It was a garish-looking abstract, painted in the cubist style in thick bright oils, although slightly faded with age. Each painting had to be valued beforehand by an expert in these matters and so it was that a certain Mr. Fleming had been brought in from Sotheby's auction house in London to give his expert opinion.

Mr. Fleming was a short rotund person with ruddy cheeks, reddish hair and small round wire-rimmed spectacles perched on his rather insignificant nose. He examined each painting with much aplomb using a magnifying glass, backlighting, direct and indirect lighting, ultraviolet light, and polarized light. His methods were time-consuming and very exacting and demanded much patience and expertise. He was most particular in noting every detail that might have the slightest bearing on the overall value of the work.

He spent a full week in Manchester until he had finished detailing the fifty works up for auction. However, something rather unusual took his eye as he was examining the Yelavich nude. Under the black light, it seemed as if there were flaws, or some kind of imperfection under the red oil paint. Upon re-examination with polarized light, he found that this was indeed the case. Mr. Fleming was taken aback when he first realized what the substance was, but upon second and third re-examinations he could only come to the same conclusion. This painting, and particularly around the lips and nipples, had been executed in blood. It was a touch-up job.

He took a deep breath and put a nervous hand to a worried brow. What was he to do? Contact the police? Without further hesitation, he did exactly that. The painting was soon in the hands of the forensic experts in the Manchester

Police Department. Polarized light microscopy was their specialty. In a week, the results were through; the blood was indeed found to be of human origin.

At once, the police were again on the Yelavich trail. They had suspected all along that it was Albert Pengally who had murdered his wife all those years ago, but Albert had never been found. This new discovery, however, put a different light on things. The new chief inspector decided to follow up his hunch and re-examine the items that were found in Albert Pengally's flat, including re-analysis of the bloodied bathwater from Caroline's last bath. The case was still open since it had never been solved.

The analysis of the DNA was done in a few days and they came up with a perfect match. The nude painting of Caroline Pengally had in actual fact been painted in her own blood—the lips and nipples in particular. The blood had then been painted over in red oil paint to disguise the fact. It was a ghoulish attempt by the artist to make a thing of beauty last forever. (The thing of beauty being his ex-fiancée, not the painting because, in Mr. Fleming's opinion, this painting would be the least valuable in the whole collection.)

Neville Yelavich's signature was found to be bona fide, as when it was analyzed by a handwriting expert, it was found to correlate exactly with some old legal archives. But the really strange thing about all this was that they discovered that the painting had been executed after Caroline's death. The techniques were so accurate now that bloodstains could be dated to within hours of their occurrence. But how could they explain this strange result? Unless…unless…The idea was unthinkable. Unless Neville Yelavich had indeed come back as a vampire to take Caroline's blood upon her death. Then, in the undead form, he would have created this garish nude of her, painted in blood, as a monument to his undying lust. It seemed incredible.

Strangely enough, when the painting was finally released for auction, there was very little bidding for it. The only flicker of interest seemed to be from a rather odd-looking and unkempt elderly gentleman with a bushy gray walrus mustache and ruddy cheeks. Apparently, he was a connoisseur of abstract art and heralded from Torquay, where he managed an antique shop. He was prepared to pay thousands for it. He certainly didn't look all that rich, but he definitely looked arty. He had that kind of thrown together look of a haunted man and his frozen fingers told all as he clutched his thick woolen scarf around his scrawny neck against the winter chill outside. He was looking forward to toasting the purchase of his precious find tonight with a nice warm mulled red wine or two…or maybe something a little stronger and more palatable from the depths of his cellar to suit his rather idiosyncratic tastes.

Little did anyone know that the reason for this little celebration lay in the fact that this was a painting of his own dear mother by his own real father, both of whom had died in very strange circumstances long, long ago.

Indeed, Dudley Pengally was so eccentric that even his own neighbors thought he was a bit strange…